ROCK

the

BEAT

(Black Falcon, #3)

MICHELLE A. VALENTINE

Table of Contents

Dedication

To the readers: You all are my cheerleaders and I love each and every one of you. If it weren't for your support I would never have the courage to keep on writing. Thank you for being so awesome!

Black Falcon Series
Reading Order

Rock the Beginning (Black Falcon, #0.5)
Rock the Heart (Black Falcon, #1)
Rock the Band (Black Falcon, #1.5)
Rock My Bed (Black Falcon, #2)
Rock My World (Black Falcon, #2.5)
Rock the Beat (Black Falcon, #3)

Coming Spring 2014
Rock My Body (Black Falcon, #4)

"It Will Rain"

Two Weeks Prior ...

For some strange reason there are socially acceptable jokes made all the time about women being late for dates, but there aren't any for guys. Take my boyfriend, Jackson Cruze, for example. He has a face like Channing Tatum, a body that David Beckham would be envious over, and the time management skills of a well-trained baboon. The guy couldn't be on time if it saves his life.

I check my watch again and sigh. Surely he wouldn't forget to pick me up tonight? We've had this date planned for our two-year anniversary for some time now. He's not that big of a jerk, is he?

I pull out my cell and call my best friend, Max, while I wait. Like clockwork, he answers on the second ring and I ask, "Where are you?"

Max laughs into the phone while the sounds of a wild party fill in behind him. "I'm at Paulo's. Why aren't you here? This is the biggest end of summer bash I've ever seen. You've got to get your ass over here."

Paulo's has the best Mexican food, drinks and DJs this side of the border. It's one of my most favorite places to hang out with my friends, and it sounds a whole lot better than waiting on my date who's already over an hour late.

I pick at my nails. "I can't. I'm waiting on Jackson. It's our anniversary."

"Um, Holly, Jackson's here."

My nostrils flare and my brow crinkles. "What?! Why is he there? He's supposed to be here." This makes no sense.

"I'm not sure, baby girl, but by the looks of him, he's been here for a while."

Un-freaking-believable. "Is he drunk?"

There's a bit of rustling on Max's end. "Judging by the number of beer cans piled on the table and slight wobble in his stance, I'd say he's hammered. Better forget tonight, Blondie, and plan on reaming his ass for it tomorrow. Come over and hang out with me. I miss you."

I resist the urge to chuck my cell out into the gravel parking lot in front of my house. Phones are expensive, and I don't have an extra penny to waste. "I'm not really feeling up to it. I think I'm going to head on to bed."

"All right. Love you. Call me tomorrow. I want to know what excuse he feeds you this time," Max says.

He's never been a big fan of Jackson's, and this little incident certainly won't help win Jackson win any favor points. I can't count the number of times Max has encouraged me to break up with my boyfriend over the last two years.

"Sure thing. Good night and have fun," I tell him before ending the call.

I haul my ass out of the old, white, rocking chair on the front porch and trudge up my stairs. I can't believe he forgot—I even reminded him today. You'd think after two years, being together with me would mean something.

I close my bedroom door and then fall onto my bed. The yellow sundress I bought special for tonight becomes my blanket as I curl my legs inside it. Tears push their way down my temples before landing in the long, mess of blonde hair spread across my pillow. I can't believe Jackson did this to me.

Don't I mean anything to him? You don't blow off people you love for a stupid party.

I know he's not been the best boyfriend in the world, but I didn't expect for him to totally blow me off like this. I know things have been rocky between us since I came home from college this summer, but that's one of the reasons I decided to stay home this fall. To mend what a year away at school had broken.

I close my eyes, feeling stupid for loving someone that obviously doesn't love me back, and cry myself to sleep.

The next thing I know my shoulder is gently shaken, stirring me out of a deep sleep. "Holly. Wake up."

It's Jackson, no doubt still drunk off his ass and feeling guilty. I roll over and rub my eyes while trying to make him out in the dark. "What time is it?"

"It's nearly five," he whispers.

I sit up quickly. "Are you out of your mind coming in here at this time of night? If my dad catches you, he'll kill you. How'd you get in here anyway?"

After blinking a few times, my vision adjusts to the moonlit room. Jackson's sitting on the edge of my bed with his lips pulled into a tight line. I tense. I've seen that look before. It's the expression he wears when he's nervous.

His polo shirt hugs his toned body as he bends at the waist, resting his elbows on his knees while he drops his head. "The front door was open, so I let myself in."

I sigh heavily. "Really, Jackson, this can't wait until the morning? I know you're sorry for standing me up. I forgive you for that.

People make mistakes."

He turns toward me and grabs my hand. "You don't know how glad I am to hear you say that. I don't want you to hate me."

I don't like the way I can sense desperation on him as he's touching me. There's something wrong. I've known him long enough that I can just feel it. "Why are you here, Jackson? Did something happen?"

Jackson runs his hand over his shaved head and shoots his gaze down at the floor. "I didn't mean to do it, Holl. You have to believe me."

I lean down trying to catch his gaze, but it doesn't work. He won't look at me and this causes my stomach to drop. "Didn't mean to do what, Jackson? You're scaring me."

He takes a deep breath. He takes a deep breath. "I've been sleeping with someone else while you were away at school, and well, I did it again tonight, so I figured it was time you knew."

My breath catches at the same time my heart crumbles in my chest. I clutch my throat. There's no air and I can't breathe. One word keeps assaulting my mind. "*Why?*"

"Because I don't think I love you anymore. If I'm being honest, I don't believe I have for a while now. We've grown apart Holly and I want to date other people." His words are barely a whisper, but he might as well be screaming them at me.

Hot tears pour down my face as I toss his hand aside. "Get out."

Jackson stands and shoves his hands deep in his jean pockets. "I'm sorry, Holl. I've wanted to tell you for a while now, but I—"

I cover my ears. I don't want to hear anything else he has to say. He's already said enough. "Get Out!"

The sound of me shouting must've been loud enough to wake my dad in his bedroom downstairs. Footsteps pound up the steps and my father comes bursting in the door with a baseball bat in hand. Panic wells in my father's eyes until he spots my boyfriend in my room, then his expression turns from fear to anger. Before Dad has a chance to scold Jackson for being in my room, Jackson runs out of my door and out of my heart for good.

Chapter One
"Closer"

Holly

I lay on my bed staring up at the ceiling. It's been two weeks since Jackson dumped me. Two weeks since my heart was obliterated. Two weeks since I basically stopped living my life. For the last two years Jackson has been my world. Without him I'm not even sure how to carry on.

A loud pounding on my bedroom door makes me jump. "Blondie, I know you're in there. Get decent, because I'm coming in."

"Max ..." I whine. "Go away. I don't want to see anybody."

The door flies open and my best friend, Max, comes barreling through. He marches over to my bed and grabs my wrist, tugging me to sit up. "Jeesh, Holly, this is pathetic. Get your cute, little ass up. We're getting you out of this house. It's been two weeks."

I groan and try to fling myself back onto my pillow, but Max's hold won't allow it. "Oh, no. No more lying in this dark room, depressed over a man that's good riddance as far as I'm concerned. You, missy, are going out and rejoining the land of the living, whether you like it or not."

I try to protest, but Max grabs my arm and leg and hoists me over his broad shoulders. "No, Max. Please."

He sighs. "Holly, this is for your own good. I'm tired of seeing you waste your energy on Jackson Cruze. He's an asshole, and I'm glad you aren't with him anymore."

"But, I love him, Max. I don't know how to live my life without him," I argue as Max carries me down the hall towards the bathroom.

Once we're in the bathroom, Max sets me down and turns on the shower before facing me. "You need to find new happiness without him. It's over between the two of you. I've already seen him with other women. Trust me, he's not pinning away over you. It's time to move on."

Tears burn my eyes of how little I actually meant to him. "He's dating already?"

Max nods and places his hands on my shoulders. "It's time for you to get back out there too. Now get your skanky ass a shower and get ready. I'm taking you to a club."

A couple hours later I find myself downtown with Max. It's *90's Nite* in one of the hottest clubs in town, and I love to dance and drink. It's the perfect combination to wipe away the memories of a man that's done me wrong.

I glance around and survey all the men in place. Why are all the really hot men either gay or taken? I swear there's one decent man left in Tucson. Thank God my best friend is with me. I have terrible gaydar.

"I told you this would be great," Max yells over the music as he dances with me to the beat of a *Roxette* song blaring through the speakers. "You'll be saying, 'Jackson who?' by the time we leave this heavenly bar filled with hot men."

I giggle and take another sip of my Sex on the Beach—compliments of Max and my fake ID. "This is a great idea—nothing like celebrating your birthday two weeks after getting dumped by the biggest jackass in the state."

Max laughs and his brown hair falls over the corner of his left eye before he takes me by the hand ready to spin me. "That was the best thing that ever happened to you, Holly. Trust me. He didn't appreciate what he had." He raises his glass of soda. "Here's to a new start in your twenties, may they be better than your teen years."

"I'll drink to that!" A tingle erupts in my hands, signaling I've nearly hit my limit, but I'm not about to let this yummy drink go to waste. Plus, it's hot in here. I down the last of it and hand Max the glass. "One more?" I give him the best pleading puppy-dog eyes I can manage.

I'm not ready to stop having fun yet. It's nice to not have to think about Jackson for a change and just have fun with my friend.

He sighs. "One more and that's it. And it's only because you're finally smiling for once in the last two weeks, but we're leaving while you can still walk out of here."

I throw my arms around his neck, leaning up on my tiptoes and kiss his cheek. "Thanks, Max. You're the bestest friend and designated driver a girl could ever have."

He laughs. "Remember how much you love me when you're praying to the porcelain god in the morning and cursing me for letting you drink so much."

"Deal," I say as I release him and go back to rocking my hips to the beat.

I fling my hair from side to side and sing along to the song, dancing like I'm alone in my bedroom instead of at a crowded bar. Normally, I'm reserved, but tonight I'm cutting loose and living up being single. I need a break from my straight-laced life.

Half way into the song, a body presses up against my back, dancing in time with me. *That didn't take long.* I tug the bottom of my little, black dress down around my thighs. The dang thing rides up every time I move and it's getting on my last nerve.

The music pumps all around me and the faceless stranger while the amount of alcohol I've consumed has my head swimming. I close my eyes and lean my head back against the hard chest behind me and breathe in the spicy scent of men's cologne. He smells mouth-watering, and I just pray that when I turn around he's as hot as I'm imagining.

The song changes and our bodies move in sync to the erotic beat of *Closer* by *Nine Inch Nails*. Trent Reznor's voice growling through the speakers about fucking causes a strange surge of arousal to come over me.

The guy behind me feels it too. Our dance turns slow and sensual as he grinds himself into my ass. His hands run down my bare arms then rest on my hips. He jerks me against him even tighter and brushes my hair to the side. I should stop him, but it's been so long since I've been touched like this, I don't want it to end. I like it too much. The feel of his nose gliding against my neck causes my mouth to drift open and I allow myself to enjoy his close proximity.

"I want to fuck you," the stranger growls in my ear before biting my earlobe.

Normally, this guy would be getting a fist to the face right about now, but because it feels amazing to have someone want me, plus I've been drinking, I'm going to allow it—if he's cute, that is.

Hell, if he's as hot as he sounds, I might just drag him into an empty bathroom stall and let him do exactly what he wants with my body.

I turn slowly, my eyes closed, praying to the hotness gods to take pity on me. My gaze lands on a toned chest wearing a tight, black t-shirt, with both of his arms covered in intricate tattoos. Good so far. My eyes travel further up and I take in the light beard on his face covering his strong jaw-line before my gaze locks on his bright green eyes. The dark hair on his head is shaggy and wild, just like the look in his eyes.

Not only is he hot, and this may be just the booze talking, but he's beautiful too. He could be possibly the hottest guy I've ever seen. I lick my lips and allow him to tighten his grip on my hips and mash me against his body even harder. My fingers dart out and run down his pecs before I wrap them around his neck and allow him to rock my body to the sensual beat of the song.

The devilish smirk he wears draws my attention to his mouth. No man should have lips that inviting, and I bite my own to keep them from attacking his. This man would be the perfect fling to take my mind off Jackson. I'm sure an hour alone with him would make me forget how pathetic I've been, pinning over a man who no longer wants me.

The beautiful stranger notices the expression on my face and, without asking permission, he leans downs and presses his lips to mine. I close my eyes and allow his greedy tongue entrance into my mouth. Every inch of my body comes alive and goose bumps erupt from my flesh as I open myself up to him.

I could do this all night—wait scratch that—I *want* to do more than this all night with him, not even caring that I don't know his name. Isn't the second person you sleep with supposed to be the complete opposite of the first? Where I'd known Jackson practically my entire life, this guy is a total stranger who seems very capable of surprising me then walking out of my life forever.

He pulls away and leans his forehead against mine. "Come home with me." My heart thunders in my chest as his tongue darts out and licks my lips before my drunken brain even has time to process his request. "I promise you'll love the way I fuck you."

I sigh heavily. If his kissing skills are any indication of what sleeping with him will be like, I have no doubt I'll love it. This is exactly what I need.

Just as I'm ready to agree, I'm jerked away, and the stranger furrows his brow, watching as I'm tugged through the crowd. Once I'm out of the hot guy's line of sight, I turn to Max, who has taken it upon himself to pull me away from a guy I was about ready to leave with.

I jerk my arm away. "What the hell are you doing?"

Max stops in his tracks, and I stagger and fall into his six-foot frame. "I'm saving your ass."

I throw my hands on my hips. "My ass didn't need saving, it needs to get laid."

Max laughs and shakes his head. "Yeah, you probably do need that. You've been extra bitchy lately."

"Hey." I smack his arm.

He wraps his arms around my shoulders and leads me up the steps to reach the bar overlooking the dance floor. Once we're up there he turns us around so we can watch the people dancing. "When you give up your cookie again, don't give it to a guy like that."

My eyes search the crowd until they land on the beautiful stranger I was just dancing with who now has that magical tongue in some blonde bimbo's mouth. I roll my eyes and wish my short legs were long enough to reach up and kick my own ass. "I'm such an idiot. Thanks, Max."

Max squeezes my shoulder. "Of course, what are friends for? You're too good for a guy like that. Don't ever date another tattooed, biker jerk like Jackson. They don't understand how special you are."

I sigh and lean my head on Max's shoulder. "Why can't you be straight? You're the perfect man for me."

He chuckles beside me. "My life would be a whole lot easier if I was. Come on. Let's get your drunk-ass home before I have to peel you off another huge mistake with a penis."

We turn and leave the club. Once outside, and away from the sexy man who had me ready to chuck everything I stand for in order to have one sinful night, I feel relieved. I have no idea how this guy had so much power over me, but at least I never have to see him again. Too much time alone with a man like him would have me breaking every personal rule I've ever set for myself. Thank God that'll never happen.

Chapter Two

"I Knew You Were Trouble"

Holly

Why the hell is it eighty-seven million degrees in this store? I know we're poor and our family business is barely staying afloat, but damn— a little air conditioning would be nice.

I re-adjust the fan on the counter, allowing the air to blow directly on me. It's disgustingly hot in here and my gray *Mountain Time Speed Track* uniform doesn't help the situation. It allows zero airflow to my skin and it's taking every bit of energy I have to not curl up under the counter and sleep off my hangover from last night.

I glance around, and when I'm sure there are no customers lurking about, I unbutton my top and stuff it under the counter. Immediately I'm relieved. The white wife-beater I have on is soaked with sweat, but at least now when the hot air whips across my skin, it feels a little cooler. Dad and I are going to have to have a serious talk about this uniform situation if he doesn't cool this place down soon. He says it adds class and professionalism when the employees have clothing assignments. Poor Dad has been implementing every "make your small business successful" tip out of all those financial magazines he's been reading lately.

I gather my long, blonde hair into a messy bun on the top of my head and grab the spray bottle I've been using to keep cool. I tip my head back, close my eyes and douse my bare skin in water. A little sigh of pleasure slips from my lips as the relief of being cool finally wafts over me.

"Damn. If I'd known I was going to see an erotic show in here I would've brought some singles with me." My eyes snap open and land on a tattooed arm in front of me holding two hundred-dollar bills. "You'll have to show a little more skin if you want me to stuff hundreds down your pants, sweetness. Only a damn good show ever earns those."

My gaze travels up the toned arm and shoulder, until it finally lands on an absurdly handsome face. A light beard covers his chin, while a baseball cap covers most of his shaggy, dark hair. His bright green eyes dance with amusement and his plump lips pull up on one side, revealing a devilish smirk. It's like the face of Adonis staring right at me and it makes my stomach flip.

Holy shit! It's him. The green-eyed devil from the club I never wanted to see again.

"Wow. *Really?*" I snatch the money from his hand a little harder than I mean to and do my best to pretend that I don't know him since he seems to have forgotten we nearly had sex last night. "How much time do you need?"

"Easy there, sugar tits, no need to be bitchy. I'm plenty fun once you lose that stick up your ass," Adonis says before winking at me.

Ugh. I bunch my eyebrows and my lip curls. What. A. Pig. And he actually has the nerve to fucking *wink* at me without mentioning something—anything—about last night?

This asshole has some balls.

This one is far worse than the typical biker boys that come here pretending like they're the next bad-ass motocross rider on earth. Those guys I can handle. They don't make my body hum with need or do something totally out of character, like sleep with a stranger.

Since Jackson broke up with me, all the guys around here have been giving me their best lines. I'm just not ready to actually date someone else. Jackson was someone I trusted. What he did nearly broke me. I'm not ready to put my heart out there again.

I've been shooting the wind out of all the proverbial sails belonging to men who have been trying to gain my attention lately. All it takes is my are-you-kidding-me-you-don't-have-a-shot-in-hell look and they turn tail and run—never looking back or giving me any more problems. Like I told Max, I'm done with guys for a while. I never *ever* want my heart broken again. Just because I let my guard down and kissed this one last night doesn't change anything. If I'd known I would ever see him again, I wouldn't have let things get that far.

Looks like I'll have to kick my bitch factor up a couple of notches to throw this one off my scent. "You look about as much fun as an albino getting sunburn. Now, how much time do you want on the track?"

"All business, aren't you?" His gaze trails up and down my body as he rakes his teeth over his bottom lip nice and slow. "You always this difficult? Because I have to say, you seem like a girl that could be a lot of fun if she let loose."

I roll my eyes and sigh, trying to decide if I can get away with cussing him out and telling him there's no chance in hell he'll ever get close to me again. Been there, done that, *so* not doing it again.

By the looks of his tattoos and bad-boy swagger, I can tell he's like all the other guys that come in here. Most never have their shit together, and still live at home with their mommies so they can play video games all day—so not attractive.

I open my mouth to tell him to give up now, but quickly close it as my father's shaking head pops into mind like my guilty little conscience. Always treat the customer with respect, even when they are rude to us—that's Dad's number one rule. So I do my best to push my personal distain for this guy out of my mind and turn on my cold indifference. "Time?"

Tattooed Adonis leans against the counter and grins. He's looking at me like he's contemplating taking me on as a challenge, so I stare back at him with raised eyebrows. "Tell me, sugar tits, did the last guy get your panties in a bunch? I'll be happy to untwist them, if you like? You'd be amazed how it'll pop that stick right out of your ass. And with a fine-ass body like yours, I'm a great volunteer and I'd consider it a public service."

My mouth gapes open and I stare at him in shock. That's it—to hell with keeping the peace in order to gain his business—this jerk has pushed me too far. "Listen here, buddy, my panties are none of your concern. As for your time, you can shove your money right up your—"

"Holly," my father scolds as he comes bursting through the front door of the shop, a scowl on his face. I sigh heavily. "I can hear you clear outside. Why are you yelling at our guest?"

The jerk focuses his eyes directly on me and smiles like a spoiled kid getting his way while waiting for me to explain to my father. "I … he … ugh! Why don't you ask *him* why?" I mutter, flinging my hands in the guy's direction. I'm so flustered I can't even speak.

I can't believe I almost slept with this guy. I'll have to kiss Max later for saving me from that giant mistake.

This stranger is frustrating, but I'm dying to see the look on his face when he tries to explain himself to Dad.

Dad scratches at the thinning hair on the top of his head nervously as he glances over at Adonis. I fold my arms across my chest while taking my turn wearing a smug grin. Adonis is so going to get it for being rude to me. My dad never lets that slide. He knows how the guys around here have been treating me lately. I know he won't stand for it.

Dad frowns and his thin shoulders sag a bit. "I'm sorry, Mr. Douglas. My daughter is normally very polite to all of our guests. Please don't inform your boss about this. I would hate to see him lose interest in partnering with the track because of Holly's momentary lack of self-control. I can assure you it's not a recurrent problem."

My mouth gapes open. Not only is my father not defending me, he's *apologizing* to the pig? I take a deep breath and allow my father's words to sink in.

Oh. Shit. "Wait. This guy? *He's* here to check out the track for the investor?"

Adonis grins even wider as he extends his tattooed arm towards me. "That's right, sugar ti—" His head snaps towards my father and he quickly clears his throat, realizing he just managed to catch himself before sexually harassing me in front of Dad. "I'm Trip Douglas. It looks like you and I will be getting cozy while you show me the ins and outs of this place."

I stare down at his hand. Ugh. This is so not happening to me. Our family business is going down the freaking toilet and I have to depend on the guy who thinks with his dick to pull us out of the hole? Maybe the investor can send someone else? *Anyone* else! No way is some rich, old dude relying solely on Trip's judgments of the place to make a huge financial commitment? This guy can't be trusted with something so important. This guy can't stick with the same woman for five minutes, let alone see such a huge business deal through.

Trip wiggles his fingers at me. "Come on. They won't bite."

Dad needs this partnership to work for the sake of the track. He told me last week how important it was for this business to get it. If it doesn't go through, we're in big trouble.

Reluctantly, I take his hand. It's warm and rough against my own skin and it's hard not to think about the way he felt pressed against me last night as he gives it a couple of quick shakes. "Holly Pearson."

He rubs his thumb across the back of my hand in slow, deliberate circles and I don't like what that little movement might be trying to imply. I've had about enough of him touching me slowly. I'm not interested now, not after I saw that I was just some random chick to him.

He smiles. "That wasn't so hard, was it?"

I roll my eyes and jerk my hand away from his grip, trying to get rid of the tingle that's left in the wake of his touch. "So what did you need again? Track time?" I quickly ask.

Trip doesn't answer—his brain obviously overloaded from his constant fixation on my chest—so I clear my throat and fold my arms, blocking his view of my boobs.

"Holly, Mr. Douglas isn't a paying customer. If he rides, it's free," Dad says.

He shakes his head like he's coming out of a daze. I didn't know my breasts could be that damn mesmerizing. "You know, Mr. Pearson, now that I've been in here, I want to start going over the books. The track test can wait for another day. It will be good to know what kind of shape this place is in financially. Everything else is fixable."

"We're actually in great shape," I snap, not liking the idea of some strange man invading our family business—especially one that I'm totally uncomfortable being in close quarters with for any period of time. I wish I hadn't liked what he'd done to me last night so damn much. "Besides, I doubt you can read them. You know they have no pictures, right?"

He leans in and braces his hands on the countertop across from me, a cool smile on his lips. "Don't let the tattoos fool you, sweetness. There's a stellar mind behind these good looks." He cocks his head to the side, giving me a look that I bet gets girls to do anything he wants. "You'll find out that I can pick a person's brain like no other. And that's why I'm here … to pick yours."

I growl and grip the counter tight to keep me from jumping over it and smacking that beautiful smile off his face. He is one smug bastard. I can't stand guys like him. It only makes it worse he's acting like he doesn't even know who I am. "You're welcome to leave any time you want. I don't need you to pick my brain or anything else connected to me or my family's business!"

"Holly!" my father warns so loudly I jump. "In my office now!"

A quick check of my dad's face tells me he's not joking around. With his eyes narrowed at me, he points his long, bony finger at his door. Even the vein in his forehead is popping out beneath his dark-brown hair. That little monster is usually reserved for when I'm in really deep shit. I stare up at Dad and nod.

I swallow hard and glance down at the counter, instantly feeling guilty for upsetting my dad. I don't enjoy disappointing him. He's got enough on his plate to worry about with the business collapsing, without having an unruly twenty-year-old daughter on his hands.

Just before I hang my head down, I glance at Trip and he frowns. I should apologize, it's the right thing to do, but with guys like him I just can't bring myself to do it. Egotistical pretty-boys think an apology is an invitation into my pants. No way do I want to give him that impression. He had his chance last night and he blew it. He won't be getting another.

I straighten my back, stiffen my shoulders and march into my father's office without giving Trip Douglas a second look.

Last year, in an attempt to bring in extra income, my dad converted his office into storage rental for customers that needed a place to store their bikes and equipment. The cramped space that was once a broom closet is now what my father calls an office. A small metal desk sits in the in the center and hogs every inch of space—and most of the oxygen—in the room. The space is what some people would consider claustrophobic. There's no relaxing view. Hell, there's not even a window, but I like it. It's quiet my escape when I need to collect my thoughts when my day gets too crazy.

The bland white walls are covered with photographs of my father smiling—pictures of him with *MX* sponsors, pro-athletes, me, Jackson and even Grace, A.K.A. my mom. Don't let the name fool you— there's nothing graceful about the woman who is nothing more than my egg donor. She's part of the reason this business is failing and why my life is slowly being sucked down the drain. The photos are a constant reminder that my once-happy life is now non-existent, which is pretty freaking depressing. Come to think of it, next time my father's out of sight I'm taking those pictures of her down and torching them. I hate being reminded of her. It's bad enough I look so much like her.

Dad follows behind me and shuts the door. After he squeezes around me, he plops down in his squeaky, green chair that's older than I am—it even has the duct-tape to prove it.

He shuffles the piles of papers around on his desk. It's the signature move he does while he gathers his thoughts—it gives the impression he's busy.

I know what he's going to say even before he does and I open my mouth to apologize, but he beats me to the punch.

"Holly, I know this is hard for you. It's hard for me too, bringing a stranger in and allowing him access to everything I've—this family—has worked so hard for all these years. I don't like it any more than you do, but these are the cards we've been dealt, honey. If this man doesn't help us, we'll lose everything." I see the sadness in his eyes as he explains.

I hear what he's saying and I completely understand, but my reservations still stick. If I could tell him why I don't think Trip can be trusted, maybe he would see my side, but I know I can't do that. Not without appearing sleazy for throwing myself at a random man in a bar. I would get the "I raised you better than that" speech. "But, Dad, *this* guy? He doesn't look like he knows anything about running a business. Did you get a good look at him? He looks like every other biker we've seen on the track, and you know they aren't always the brightest crayons in the box."

Dad drags his fingers through his thinning hair. His hair, like the rest of his body is withering away. He's lost so much weight over the last couple months—it makes his six-foot-two frame seem even taller. The stress is really getting to him. "Holly, I know what this place means to you. I'm grateful that you left school and to come home and help me out, but this place isn't your cross to bear. It's mine. This place is *my* dream, and it makes me feel like I failed as your father because I willingly allowed you to throw away *your* dream of finishing college to come back here to help me. If I can just get this place back into the black you can go back to school, like you planned. Convincing Trip to get this investor on board will make that happen. You can get your life back."

I frown as I walk around the desk and wrap my arms around my father. "Dad, I made the choice to come back here because I wanted to. You were here, and Jackson. You and this track are my life. Just because I'm not with Jackson anymore doesn't mean I regret my decision. I love it here. This place is my home and I want to help in any way I can to save it." Dad smiles. "Besides, I can always get a loan once we get this place back on its feet. Ohio State isn't going anywhere any time soon. It's you and me. And we stick together."

He folds his arms around me and pats the back of my head. "We do make a pretty great team, don't we? Since your mom left—"

I stiffen in his embrace and cut him off before he goes down memory lane about Grace. "Let's not talk about her."

Dad sighs as I pull away and lean back against the desk. "All right but, honey, please try and be civil to Trip. I really want this to work out. We *need* him to like us."

I roll my eyes. As much as it kills me, I know I have to play nice. "I'll try, but I swear if he comes on to me like the rest of the goons around here, I promise I won't show any mercy."

He chuckles. "I would expect nothing less from you. Just please don't rip his head off. I can't afford a lawsuit. I'm trying to get money from him, not give it."

We both laugh because it's no secret around this track that I'm quick witted and unafraid to put any man in his place. I'm one tough, general operations manager. This may be a male-dominated sport, but at *Mountain Time Speed Track* it's most definitely a woman's world.

Trip

I rub my forehead, wishing I could take back the last five or so beers past my limit I drank last night. Walking into this place with a hangover wasn't the brightest idea I've ever had. Thank God Mr. Pearson wasn't insistent I check out the track first. I would've puked after the first five minutes of riding.

I didn't mean to get that hot blonde in trouble with her dad. Flirting with beautiful women mercilessly is my favorite past time. I can't help myself. And Holly Pearson is one fine piece of ass. No doubt about that. She reminds me a lot of that blonde I kissed last night, or at least I think I kissed last night. Things started getting hazy after my tenth drink, or maybe it was the twelfth drink. Alcohol has a way of fucking up my brain and making shit a blur. The blonde was smoking hot too. One minute she was grinding her ass against my dick, causing me nearly to come in my jeans, the next minute she was gone, dragged off by another guy. Lucky bastard was probably her boyfriend.

So, I had to find some random chick. I couldn't let a good hard-on go to waste. One of these nights I'm going back to that club while I'm in town to find that girl. It's a shame her face is kind of a blur today.

I glance up at the clock on the wall. Mr. Pearson and Holly have been gone for nearly ten minutes and there's no sign of them coming out any time soon.

Holly is really feisty. I'm going to have to figure out a way to make her my friend if I'm going to be here for the next four weeks. I hate tension. It bugged the fuck out of me when Noel and Riff fought. I'm so glad that shit's over. That kind of shit wears on a persons sanity after a while, which is why I need to squash whatever problem Holly has with me. Most women giggle and love it when I put the moves on them. It's an ego boost to them. But this one loathes me and I don't have a fucking clue why.

It's totally obvious she has no clue who the hell I am because she seemed rather appalled by me, which *never* happens. Most people turn into over-pleasing twits around celebrities. It's fucking annoying not to be able to get the truth out of people.

I drum my fingers on the countertop, tapping out the beat of a new song my twin brother and band-mate, Tyke, and I have been working on for the past couple weeks. With a few minor tweaks I think we'll have the next Black Falcon hit-single ready to record when we finally head back into the studio next month.

I really miss working. Black Falcon and the rest of the guys are my life. I love everything about my job, and I don't mean to toot my own horn, but I consider myself the best fucking drummer in the business. I can pound out grungy, raw beats like nobody in the business, and the combination of my beats and Tyke's bass flowing in sync creates magic that's often emulated, but never duplicated. No one can rock the beat like we can. Black Falcon is unique and our bond as a band is stronger now than ever before. It might make me a pussy for saying this but I'll admit, when we're not all together I feel a little homesick.

If it weren't for women getting in the way of our work, we'd be on the road right now touring. The whole situation pisses me off a bit.

Yeah, I know. Sure, Lane and Aubrey are great chicks and have done wonders in getting Noel and Riff to settle down and become friends again, but it doesn't mean they aren't cramping the rest of our styles. It's been over a month since I banged a random groupie and I hate this fucking dry-spell. It makes me edgy, which is why I had to go out to a club in Tucson last night and find a random piece of ass. I needed to take the edge off.

The thought of throwing Holly down on this counter and fucking her seven different way from Sunday entered my head about a thousand times during our little heated discussion. Girls with attitude are hot and she's exactly my type—a petite blonde with perfect tits. Even when she was mean as hell to me, all I could think about was

24

kissing that rude mouth of hers.

See what I mean? I can't function without sex—it's like a fucking drug. I'm used to getting it daily, and when you don't get what you crave, you'll find your fix wherever you can. Which is why that lay last night, even as lousy as it was, was a blessing. I was at least able to keep why I was actually here on my mind and not be completely distracted by those perky, little tits of Holly's.

Going undercover at this dirt bike racing track, looking at it as a potential investment will be good for me. I need to branch out a bit. I've gotten bored with all the time off Noel and Riff have need lately. Both of them decided to run off and start families—I get it—but that does nothing for me. I need something else to occupy my time. If I'd had to sit in the house with my brother and work on one more song I swear to God I would've gone nuts. Noel and Riff are killing me with their need for all this personal time off.

What about *me*? What about *my* needs?

I say drag those strollers on the tour bus and let's get the fuck back on the road where the action is.

I can't see myself ever settling down with one woman for the rest of my life. Not because I couldn't mind you, but because I don't want to. *That* lifestyle is for pussies. Fuck the estrogen-induced life Riff and Noel are leading.

I've tried monogamous dating before and that shit went horribly wrong. Never again. NEVER. It's just not for me. How does that saying go—burn me once, or some shit?

The office door swings open without warning and I straighten my stance. Holly comes out first just as the circulating fan blows in her direction. Fallen strands of her blonde hair whip back off her face and she sets her blue eyes on me. For some reason the sight of her hits me like a rock video set in slow motion. I mean, I noticed she was sexy before, but from this angle I've got a hell of a view.

Her long, slender legs move her voluptuous body right to me. There's a confidence in her step that's undeniable and makes her really fucking sexy. Sure, there are women who would turn any man's head around me all the time, but this one has something special. Too special for someone like me, but it still sort-of hurts my ego that she turned me down. I'm not used to that.

Holly walks around the counter to face me and I smile. As much as I wouldn't mind fucking this girl, I need to keep my dick in my pants. I need her on my side—sleeping with her would only complicate the hell out of this business deal.

No way do I want to deal with a woman I've one-nighted for years to come. That's just bad for business.

She sighs and holds out her hand. "I think we got off on the wrong foot, and I'd like us to start over. I'm Holly."

I take her dainty little hand into mine, and as much as my dick is urging me to use my typical game on her, I refrain. I squeeze her hand and give it a couple firm shakes. "Trip Douglas. I look forward to working with you, Holly."

Her eyes narrow for a split-second, but as soon as I let go of her hand and shove both of mine deeply in my pockets to show her I'm done trying to be touchy-feely, her expression changes and a polite smile touches her lips.

She's got a great fucking smile.

As my fingers itch to touch her soft skin again, I roll them into fists and fight the urge. As hot as I think she is, nothing can ever happen with her. I can't give into the want I feel for her.

"Can we go over the books later? I was actually getting ready to grab lunch," Holly says. "We can start afterwards."

"Great," Mr. Pearson says as he comes out of the office. "Holly can show you to your room when she gets her lunch."

Her head whips in his direction. "What do you mean *his* room?"

Mr. Pearson frowns at Holly. "I forgot to mention that part, honey. Trip will be staying in the guest room while he's here. We talked about it when I showed him around earlier. It'll be good for him to be with us and see how we operate this family business."

She opens her mouth to protest about me staying in her home, but quickly closes it when her dad tilts his head and slides his gaze toward her. Mr. Pearson was kind enough to offer me a place to stay while I'm here checking out the track. He wanted me to feel welcome and expressed to me how much he hopes this deal works out.

Their family house is located on the same property as the track, literally a stone's throw from the office. It'll save me from having to drive back and forth from that shitty hotel I stayed in last night. Besides, it'll be nice not to live in a hotel for once while I'm on the road.

I watch Holly fidget. I can tell the idea of me staying with them makes her uncomfortable. That's not a good sign if I want my plan of making her like me to work. "Mr. Pearson, it's fine. I don't mind staying at the hotel."

He dismisses me with a wave of his hand. "Don't be silly, son. Staying in a hotel is pricey. Do you know what a month's stay would cost? We have a spare room and we'd be happy to have you. Besides, Mr. Johnson from the bank already has my contact information and knows that he can contact you here for updates. I want your boss to know we are a trustworthy family."

Shit. I forgot about that. Does it make me a tool for lying to them about the fact that I'm really the investor? I hope not. I'm not doing it to be cruel. It's just important to me to keep my identity concealed. I want to see how my money will be used on a daily basis. I don't want any special treatment getting in the way of that.

When I sent my investment banker on the quest to find me a business opportunity involving motocross, I couldn't have been more pleased when he found me this sinking diamond in the rough. Mr. Pearson has fallen behind on his payments and the bank is only a couple of months away from foreclosing. It was once a lucrative business, but for some reason, over the last couple of years, business has drastically declined. That's why I'm here. I want to figure out what makes this place tick, discover if my money can help fix it up and put this place back on the map as a premier training facility for riders.

But, I don't want the Pearson's to know all that. For the time being I'm happy having them think that I'm just some biker sent here by their bank.

I nod, believing that, in order to play my role of a poor biker guy, staying with them is best. "Okay then. Sounds great. I already have my things in the car, anyhow. The place I stayed in last night had the most uncomfortable bed. I planned on finding a new one today."

"Fantastic. Honey, would you mind showing Trip his room," Mr. Pearson says with a sparkle of excitement in his eyes.

Holly sighs heavily before saying, "Come on. Follow me."

Mr. Pearson smiles at Holly like a proud father. That must've been some talk in that office. Before I turn to leave, I extend a hand to him. "Thanks again for having me out, Mr. Pearson. I know the investor is really excited about the business."

Our hands clap together on contact. "Call me Bill. Mr. Pearson was my father."

I laugh. "Fair enough."

Bill asks, "What's your boss like? Mr. Johnson wouldn't tell me much about him—only that he's a man with a lot of money itching to get his hands into something dealing with motocross."

Bill seems like a nice guy, and he would probably be okay with who I am. I seriously doubt he's a fan and so he wouldn't flip his shit if he found out, but I resist spilling my secret. I simply shrug. "He's a good guy. I've known him all my life, but he prefers to keep a low profile. My friend recently came into a lot of money. He loves the outdoors and thought this business would be a great fit with his adventurous streak. He knows I like to ride bikes and that I'm good with business and large dollar amounts, so he asked me to come here and check out the place. I've got his information and, after the month is over, I'll report back to him with my opinion."

He nods. "It's nice to know we're dealing with a decent guy. For a minute there I was starting to worry he was some big name celebrity who really wouldn't give a crap about wanting to turn this place around."

That makes me laugh and I shake my head. Bill Pearson may be smarter than I initially thought. "You're right. Celebrities are a pain in the ass. But trust me when I say my friend has the best of intentions when it comes to this place."

I turn towards Holly, who is waiting for me patiently by the front door.

I pull my ball cap down further over my brow to cover more of my face and slip outside with a girl who I'm convinced hates me. That is, until she looks at me and smiles.

It's then I notice that not only is she hot, but she's beautiful. I mean, I knew she was pretty, but out here with the sunlight on her hair, wearing a smile that could light up the entire fucking world, my breath actually fucking catches. I shake my head to clear all those sappy thoughts away. What the hell is wrong with me? I don't think like that. Ever. If I ever said something like that around the guys, I would never hear the fucking end of it.

The expression on her face fades just as quickly as it appeared as she catches me shaking my head because I'm disgusted with myself. "Dad likes you. I hope you're a good guy and do right by him and this place."

Great. She probably thinks I was being a jackass or something. If I told her the truth about why I was shaking my head, it would be ten times worse. I need to keep myself in check and remind myself to stay focused. Seeing Holly Pearson naked, moaning my name below me can never happen.

Chapter Three

"Rude Boy"

Holly

The metal keys feel like lead in my hand as I pull them from my pocket to let us into the house. The idea of sleeping under the same roof as this sexy man makes me feel a little uneasy. Even though I would never allow anything to happen between us, it doesn't stop my eyes from lingering on him longer than they should—I'm only human and I'm not blind. I'm going to admire the view even though I know his breed of asshole is bad news. I've seen the way he is with women and I will not allow myself to be some conquest to him.

"This is a nice place," Trip says from behind me as I twist the key and push the door open.

"Thanks. It's not much, but it's home," I answer politely and glance over my shoulder at him, knowing he's only saying that to be nice.

Trip stares up, studying the rafters in our unfinished porch. The idea that he's judging us on the looks of the place makes me stiffen. Like most things around here, Dad never had the time or money to get around to actually completing it. Not that he doesn't want to, but things cost money, and that's one thing we haven't had very much of in a while. At the rate we've been going, we're lucky to keep the electricity on.

I open the door wide and step back. "Welcome."

He smirks and shakes his head before sweeping his hand out in front of him. "Ladies first."

I roll my eyes and shrug. I flip on the light in the small foyer as Trip closes the door. Even though it's two in the afternoon, we still have to waste electricity running the lights all day because of how dark it stays in this old farmhouse. I was just a baby when Grace, and Dad bought this place. It had been a fixer-upper, but had all the potential for my dad to realize his dream of opening a dirt-bike track. Twenty years later it still needs a lot of fixing.

As a kid, the condition of this place used to embarrass me, but now that I'm older and understand the concept of money, I'm just glad we have a roof over our head. I don't care what people think about me anymore.

"How long have you lived here?" Trip asks as he walks around, peeking his head in the living room and the kitchen to inspect the place.

"All my life." My feet find the first step on the staircase. "Your room is up here."

His eyes follow the staircase to the second level. "I was thinking, why not start with a tour of your room instead?"

I shake my head as he follows me up the stairs. "That's never going to happen."

He laughs behind me. "If denying how much you want me makes you sleep better at night, have at it."

At the top of the landing I turn around and Trip stops one step below me, so our eyes are level. I'm about two seconds from ripping into him and telling him how disgusted I am that he doesn't even remember me, but I decide if he's going to play dumb, than so am I. "There are two bedrooms up here. The door to your right is mine, and the door on the left is yours. The door at the end is the bathroom. We'll have to share it."

His green eyes dart from one side of the hall to the other, checking out the tan walls and white doors with caution. "So it's just the two of us up here alone?"

I tilt my head and narrow my eyes. "Is that going to be a problem for you?"

He sets his foot on the top step and leans into me a bit, closing the gap between us. "Not for me, but can't say the same for you."

I fold my arms under my boobs, drawing his attention to my chest again. I could kick myself right now for not putting my uniform top back on. "Why would that be a problem for me?"

Trip smirks. "Don't think I haven't noticed you giving me the old fuck-eye. I'd say in a week or so I'll have to keep my door bolted shut to keep you from sneaking in and having your way with me."

I let out a bitter laugh. What a self-centered jerk. "Don't flatter yourself. You're not my type."

He studies my face. After a few seconds he raises his eyebrows as it appears he's had a flash of memory, because a gleam of recognition flashes in his eyes. "You sure about that? It didn't seem that way last night."

The blood drains from my face. Shit. He *does* remember. "That was a drunken mistake. I wasn't myself last night. Trust me that won't be happening again anytime soon."

"I told you, sweetness, I can read people. It's sort of my thing. Sooner or later you're going to have to admit to yourself that you're into me. I drank a lot at the bar and I thought you looked like the girl from last night, but I wasn't sure. Not until just now, that is. In this dark hallway, you look just the same as you did last night. You wanted me too. I know you did. I could feel it in your kiss."

"Like I said. You've got no chance in hell with me."

"Really?" He laughs heartily and steps onto the landing in front of me and his face is suddenly serious. "I'd say you were pretty damn close to allowing me to have my way with you last night. If your boyfriend hadn't dragged you away, we would've had a great time. Where is he now, anyway?"

"My love life isn't your concern." He steps closer to me and I shake my head and take a step backwards. He's trying to bait me into playing his game by closing the distance. "This isn't going to work on me, you know."

Trip scrunches his brow. "What isn't?"

I wave my hands in front of me, directing attention to his body. "This ... your whole bad-boy charm. I'm immune to it. I don't sleep with guys I don't know."

He traces a line down my arm with his finger. "Sweetheart, I haven't even begun to charm you yet. When I do, I promise I won't have to ask twice to get you naked. You'll be begging for me to take you and make your body feel good, just like you were last night."

I roll my eyes and try to pretend my heart isn't pounding fifty miles an hour. "You are so full of shit."

He licks his lip, and stares into my eyes so intensely I bite the inside of my cheek to keep from making any noise while under his powerful gaze. "I know you're trying real hard to make yourself believe what you're saying. Honestly, I find your self-preservation charming. But I happen to know women are defenseless when I set out to seduce them."

I lift my chin. "I highly doubt you can get any woman you want. I hope that's not what you're trying to do with me, because if it is, I can assure you, you're failing miserably."

"When I decide I want something, I get it. Always. Failure isn't in my vocabulary."

The determination in his eyes makes my legs weak. There's no doubt in my mind he can get *most* women to do whatever he wants when there's pure alpha male radiating from him. But I'm not most women, and he won't be making me another notch on his undeniably sexy bedpost any time soon.

He takes another step. "Admit that you like me."

I shake my head as he takes another step, followed by another until my back is pinned against the wall. "No."

Trip bites his lip and leans into me and places two fingers against my neck like he's checking my pulse. "Then tell me, sweetness. Why is your heart racing? You can deny it all you want, but you'll only be able to fight what your body wants for so long."

My breath catches. He makes me nervous and I don't like the effect he's having on me. I wish he was wrong about my stupid body wanting him.

I clear my throat and shove myself away from him, needing to get away from him. "If you need anything other than sexual favors you just let me know."

Before he can say anything else, I slip into my room and close the door behind me. I press my back into the door and sigh. Damn, I wish he wasn't right. I do feel some strange pull toward him, but I'll be damned if I give in to it and get my heart broken again.

I stay still until I hear his footsteps go back downstairs and then the front door shut. I slide down the door and take a deep breath. Trip is more intense than I'm used to. Sure, in a place overrun with men, guys come onto me all the time, but this one? He's different. I've never had a man so sure of himself approach me like that. Most guys in come into the shop and tell me I'm hot or have a great ass and then get pissed when I don't drop my panties fast enough for them.

I'm done dating jerks.

I have to put a tougher bubble in place around me. This guy isn't going to take no for an answer, which may be a problem seeing as how I have to be in close proximity to him for a month. That, and the fact that he's quite possibly the most attractive man I've ever laid eyes on.

Before I have time to think on it any further, my cell phone whistles with a text message.

Kara: Missed you at the Alpha Gamma Sigma party. These things aren't the same without you.

I smile as I read her message. Kara is a girl I met back at Ohio State. We were a package deal last year when it came to parties. I hate the fact that I dropped out of college after my spring semester was over this year. I hoped Kara and I would be together my entire time there seeing as how we were both studying to be psychologist.

Holly: Miss you too. How is everyone?

Kara: Everyone is exactly the same. Summer break didn't change things much.

Holly: Tell them I said hello.

Kara: Will do. Has Jackson begged for your forgiveness yet?

Holly: No, he's been keeping his distance and only talking to me when he has business at the track.

Kara: He deserves a swift kick in the balls for what he did to you.

The thought of Jackson and what he did to me makes my blood boil. The last thing I want to do right now is think about him. For the last two weeks it's been torture seeing him around the town knowing how he betrayed me. For once I wish there was another track in town he could train on. He hasn't been to the track since that night in my room, but I know he can only stay away so long. He has to have a place to train seeing as he's becoming a professional rider.

Holly: Agreed.

My answer is simple. I hope it's enough to pacify her so she will drop the topic.

I sigh in relief as her next text comes through.

Kara: Gotta get to class. Miss you! XOXOX

I shove myself off the floor and stuff my phone back in my pocket. Kara's text couldn't have come at a better time. The mention of Jackson only solidifies the need for me to be done dating guys for a while. And by *a while* I mean probably forever. I just can't trust them, and if I can't trust them why would I hand over something as precious as my heart? They'll just destroy it for the hell of it.

Especially someone like Trip Douglas. He has heartbreaker written all over him. I would like nothing more than to completely ignore him with the hope that he and his sexy body disappear. I'm going to have to fight hard to deny him considering I've already tasted his lips and my body already wants him—a woman can only be so good for so long.

After eating my lone peanut butter sandwich, I decide it's time to go back to the main office. As much as I would like to, I can't avoid Trip forever.

I lock the front door behind me and the gravel crunches under my feet as I trudge towards the office.

Like everything else around here, this building has seen better days. The posts on the front porch could use a fresh coat of paint and the building itself needs a few upgrades. The red brick is dull and dingy, with some of the mortar between them cracking and peeling away. The bushes are in great shape though thanks to a day's worth of sweat from me out here trimming them up. I remember that day fondly. I saw Jackson at the local mall talking to Stella Charles, the girl I'd recently heard he'd been sleeping with all last year while I was away at college. I took all my aggression out on our poor shrubbery that day.

Max leans against the porch railing in his black and yellow riding gear as I approach. "A little late for work aren't you? How many times did you barf?" Max asks as I close in on him.

I give him my best scowl. "A couple, thanks to you."

He laughs and his brown, floppy hair bounces. I stick my tongue out at him and his brown eyes grow wide before he rushes over and grabs me up in a big bear hug. "Is that any way to treat your best friend who was trying to break you out of a funk on your birthday?"

I smack his chest as I try to wiggle out of his hold. "Who said you were my best friend? I should hate you for how much you let me drink last night."

Max sets me down and dramatically throws his hands over his heart. "That wounds me deeply, Holly. It's not like I didn't warn you."

I pull his hands down. "Stop it. You know I'm kidding. What girl wouldn't want a best friend as handsome as you?"

He gives me a lopsided grin. "That's more like it. Have you seen the new man-meat in the shop? He looks a lot like that guy from last night, only today he's got a hat on."

I shrug and toss my blond hair over my shoulder. "It is the same guy. Good thing I didn't sleep with him, huh?"

His eyes widen. "Holy shit! What's he here for? Did he track you down?"

I shake my head. "He's here to inspect the track for that investor Mr. Johnson told Dad about."

Max raises his eyebrows. "Really? He's not exactly what I expected."

"You're preaching to the choir. He's a real piece of work too—so full of himself. The Gods-gift type, you know. I owe you one for saving me from him last night."

He folds his arms over his chest. "You telling me we have another Jackson on our hands?"

Jeesh, does *everyone* have to bring up Jackson today? "Ugh. I hope not. Trip claims to actually have a brain."

Max grimaces. "Trip? What in the hell kind of name is that? Who would do that to a kid?" I stay quiet and he notices. "You don't think it's a weird name?"

"I don't know. It's not so bad."

"What?" Max bends down to look me in the eye. "Wait a minute. You *like* him. I thought we talked about this last night?"

I open my mouth to protest but Max's laugh cuts me off, and I grimace before arguing. "I do not."

I start to turn away as the heat rises in my cheeks, but he grabs my arm. "Oh no you don't. Don't deny it—you're into him. How quickly you forget that I've seen that look on your face before. Admit it. You got a thing for him. You still want to bang him, don't you?"

I shake my head and shove his shoulder playfully. "Maybe it's you that has a thing for him."

His face gets pale. He hates it when I hint at his sexual preference within earshot of others. After he whips his head from side to side, making sure no one overheard, he sets his eyes on me. "Sometimes I wish that you didn't know so much about me."

I grin, knowing I'm the only one who knows his little secret. "You know that's exactly why you love me."

He wraps his arm around me and turns in plain view of the window looking into the shop where we can get a clear view of Trip. "That's way too much man for you, Holly. A guy like that will chew you up and spit your little heart all over the sidewalk. You need to steer clear of that tasty piece of dangerous ass."

I roll my eyes. "Seriously? When have I ever been interested in that type?"

"Oh, I don't know. Maybe since high school?"

"I'm completely over Jackson Cruze, and the bad-boy type. I was drunk last night and my judgment was off. I promise I won't be letting my guard down again."

"Really? After one day? Why do you still have those magazine covers of him hanging on your walls?"

"He's the hottest motocross rider around. It's good for our business when people find out that he trains here at this track," I argue.

Max gives me a pointed look. "Keep telling yourself that, Blondie."

I shrug his arm off my shoulder. "Ugh. Whatever. Let's not talk about Jackson anymore."

He smirks. "Why? Got your eye on someone new?"

"I told you, I don't like him!" I gesture towards the window where we last saw Trip.

Shit.

At the same moment I realize Trip is gone, a voice behind me stops me dead in my tracks. "I hope you're not talking about me. You'll break my heart if you are."

I could kill Max right now. I narrow my eyes at my best friend and do my best to send him a telepathic message that he's dead meat before turning to face Trip, wearing the sweetest smile I can muster. Against my better judgment, I have to force myself to be nice to this guy. Like Dad said, we need him to like us. "Of course not. I don't even know you well enough to not like you yet."

He leans casually against the doorframe that leads inside the office. The rickety screen door is propped open with a red brick to allow more airflow into our hot-as-hell office, giving me a full view of Trip and that mouth-watering body of his. I jerk my eyes off his chiseled, tattoo-covered biceps and he chuckles. Damn it. He caught me looking. I have *got* to get his sexiness out of my mind.

Trip's eyes flit to Max, like he's testing to see if my gay best friend is my actually my boyfriend before deeming it safe to turn his heated gaze in my direction.

I glance over at Max and he holds up his hands, indicating he has no ties to me as Trip stares him down. Trip shifts his heady gaze from Max to me. "Well, I'm all for rectifying that problem."

I shake my head. "You don't take *no* for an answer very well, do you?"

"Not when it comes to something I want."

I laugh. "And I'm guessing I'm something you want?"

He shrugs. "Maybe, I'm still making up my mind. Don't worry, as soon as I decide, you'll be the first to know."

This guy does not give up. "Well, like I said, you and I are never going to happen. I'm not sleeping with you. You might as well get that idea out of your head right now. But whenever you'd like to go over the business aspects of the place, I'm all for it."

I start to shoulder around him to get inside the office, but he grabs my wrist, halting me in my tracks, and the look in his eyes softens. "I'm sorry. I don't mean to piss you off. From now on, I'll be a perfect gentleman. I want us to be friends."

I stare up into his green eyes and take in his easy smile. He bites his bottom lip and all I can think about is how soft his lips were when he kissed me. I silently curse myself for thinking about his stupid mouth before I shake out of his grip. "Good. Come on, then."

Chapter Four
"Good Girls, Bad Guys"

Trip

I turn my head and watch Holly stalk off inside. I fold my arms over my chest and blow a frustrated breath through pursed lips. This isn't good.

"She doesn't hate you if that's what you're thinking," the guy she was talking to says to me. I turn my gaze in his direction and he extends his right hand to me. "The name's Max."

I grip his hand in mine and give it a firm shake. "Trip."

Max nods. "So I've been told."

I ask the question that's been burning in my brain since I placed him as the guy who'd dragged Holly away from me last night. "You her boyfriend or something?"

He grimaces and shakes his head like I've just insulted him. "God no. We're just friends."

Just friends I can work with. He must be gay. Any red-blooded guy would be proud to own up to tapping an ass like Holly's, but … whatever.

I'm so glad she wasn't my random fuck last night, although I bet she would've been ten times better than what I ended up with.

Damn it.

I have to stop thinking about her that way. She's not some random chick I'll never see again. There's no 'hump and dump' option here. I need her on my side in order to get the low-down on this place. I can already tell she's the key to making this a successful business venture.

I glance back in Holly's direction and watch as she piles a bunch of binders on the counter. She doesn't even look in my direction. "What makes you so sure she doesn't hate my guts?"

Max grins wider than the Cheshire cat. "I was there last night. My girl in there doesn't just let any guy get his lips on her. If she didn't like you, she would've kneed you in the balls the moment you came on to her. Granted, she was drunk last night, and she's going through some things, but she still allowed you to kiss her."

I look him directly in the eye. "You seem awfully protective. You sure you're not into her?"

He shakes his head. "She's my best friend and I watch out for her. I don't like to see her get hurt because she's a good person and deserves better than what she's been dealt lately. Holly's a tough woman, but she's also sweet and sensitive. If you aren't sincere in your intentions toward her, I'm asking you to back off. She's not ready for more heartbreak."

I open my mouth to ask what he meant by that exactly when Holly calls my name. "Trip, you coming or not? I don't have all day."

Max takes a couple steps back. "I'm sure I'll see you around."

I nod as his words of warning flow through my mind. "Later, man, and thanks."

"No problem. Good luck." He laughs as he hops on his dirt bike and fires up the motor.

Inside, the stifling air is hard to ignore, but now I understand why they don't turn the air on. Their business is failing and they need to save every penny they can. I yank my ball cap off and wipe the sweat off my forehead with the back of my wrist. The entire state of Arizona is hot as hell.

Holly's eyes train on my hair and her lips twist. "Do you dye your hair? I didn't notice how black it was last night."

She leans over the counter to fetch the schedule. I eye her daisy-duke covered ass appreciatively while her head's turned. If she catches me eye-fucking her, she'll smack the shit out of me, but it's worth the risk. Her ass is one hundred percent biteable and I curse myself for wanting a piece.

I run my hand through my hair, pushing it back off my face before slapping my hat back on. "Yeah. I like it jet-black. It helps people tell me and my twin brother apart."

She tilts her head and leans on the counter across from me. "Is he identical?"

I nod. "He is, except for the hair. His is more of a sandy-blond color."

"Huh." The look on her face tells me she's trying to figure out why I color my hair. Or worse, she's figuring out who I am.

"You've got something on your mind."

"No ... well, yes. I was wondering something."

"What's that?"

She clears her throat. "I can see wanting to stand out from your brother when you're little to help people tell you apart, but why do feel the need to do it as an adult?"

I sigh in relief. I was fully prepared for her to ask me about Black Falcon. "We work together."

Her eyebrows crunch together. "Does he work for the same investor too?"

Fuck. Panic floods over me as I realize my slip up. Quickly, I try to cover my mistake. "No. I'm working for the investor as a favor. He and I are personal friends. My brother and I have our own business."

"Doing what?"

"We, um ..." I trail off, trying to think of a plausible lie. "Our family owns a ..." —I glance around the counter and the cowtail candies catch my eye— "farm."

She flinches at the same time I want to punch myself in the face for saying something so ridiculous. "What kind of farm?"

I don't know the first thing about farming. Why in the fuck did I say that?

Holly stares at me expectantly and I clear my throat. "Cows. We farm cows."

I want to fucking kill myself.

"Really?" She raises her brow. "Like a dairy farm? I've never seen a farmer look like you before."

I nod. Milk, yes. That's something I know about. I've seen people milk cows before on television not to mention I eat a ton of cereal and milk. "Yes, exactly like a dairy farm. We go out and milk the cows every morning by hand."

She laughs. "Nice try. You almost had me for a minute. I know they get hooked up to machines for milking. I've seen that in a movie before. I didn't know you had a sense of humor."

I laugh too but it's fake as hell, and I pray she can't hear the nervousness in my voice. "There's no fooling you."

She leans across the counter with a smirk on her pretty pink lips. Without knowing she's doing it, she gives me a perfect view of her boobs. "There's a stellar mind behind these good looks, sweetheart,"

Holly says while lowering her voice to imitate me.

Wow. Now she's throwing my own lines back in my face, making me sound like a complete fucking moron. "Good one."

Holly straightens her stance and pats her hand on the stack of black binders. Each one has enough papers to fill a phone book. "Come on, genius. We've got a lot of books to go over."

I eye the stack and frown. "It's all on paper?"

She nods. "Dad didn't know how to work a computer when he started this place and never got around to converting all the books. Besides, computers cost a lot of money."

I run my hand over my face. "This is going to take *forever*."

She shrugs. "I know, so we might as well get going. The faster we get through all this, the quicker you can convince your boss this is a great place to invest in."

It takes at least an hour for Holly to explain the set-up of all the paper documents and then another hour before I can even begin making sense of their system. No wonder this business is going to shit. There's not even an accurate way to track the expenses. Apparently there are also shoeboxes full of receipts that Bill has never gotten around to adding into the budget. This is so not good. Updating the computers alone in this place is going to cost a pretty penny. I can only imagine what the track looks like. I'll have to look into that tomorrow.

Holly interlocks her fingers and stretches her arms above her head, allowing the gray uniform top she's wearing to ride up and bit and give me a peek at her toned stomach. "I need a break. What about you?"

I fold the page over in the book I'm reading through and rub my eyes. "I'm starving. Where's a good place to eat around here?"

"If you drive into town, there are a few places."

I tilt my head. "You don't want to come with me?"

She shakes her head. "There's stuff to make peanut butter sandwiches in the house."

I knit my brow in confusion. "Peanut butter sandwiches for dinner?"

"Why not? It's cheap and filling," she argues.

I stand and find that my ass is all sweaty from sitting on the black, plastic stool for such a long period of time. "You aren't eating that. Get your ass up. You're coming to dinner with me."

She frowns. "Really, I can't go. I can't afford it."

Now I feel like a total jackass. "My treat. I've been a jerk to you since I got here. The least I can do is buy you dinner to make up for it. We can go anywhere you want."

She drops her eyes to the counter while she thinks it over. "Okay. But this doesn't change what I said earlier. I still won't sleep with you."

"I haven't asked you to, have I?"

"Well … not in those exact words, but your actions—"

I grab her arm and haul her up off the stool. "Like I told you, if I intended on fucking you, you'd know it. Now quit talking nonsense and come on. I'm so hungry I'm about to gnaw my arm off."

I don't give her much choice in the matter. The caveman in me comes out and I pull her behind me out the door.

The sun setting over the mountainside helps cool down the intense September heat, but it doesn't change it that drastically. Now instead of one hundred and five degrees, it's a balmy eighty-eight. Whoever told me the high temperatures in Arizona were a different kind of heat to Kentucky was fucking loony. Eighty-eight is still fucking eighty-eight. It's the kind of heat where it feels like a furnace is blowing directly on you and your balls stick to your leg. It's fucking uncomfortable.

I continue to pull Holly along until we reach a black Mustang parked around back.

"WOW! How much do you make working for this investor? That car is beautiful." Holly twists out of my hold and begins walking around the car slowly. "Is this a two thousand fourteen—a V-8?"

She runs her hand along the hood, caressing the sleek paint job. "I think so. It's not mine. It's a rental. I'm not much of a car fanatic. As long as it's fast, I like it."

Her head snaps up in my direction and her eyes widen. "Most guys won't let anyone touch their baby, but since it's not technically yours, will you let me drive it? I've always wanted to test one of these babies out."

The gleam in her eye is the same one I get when I get a new set of drums, or find a hot piece of ass. When something you really want is within your grasp it's easy to get that look of awe on your face. Fuck me. I never imagined a car would turn her on. It's the first time I've ever seen a woman get hot and bothered by a car.

"Sure." I toss the keys over the hood and she catches them with quick, nimble fingers. "Anything to relieve that lady-boner of yours."

"I should say you're a perv for that remark, but since you're letting me drive this beautiful machine, I'll let that one slide." A genuine smile toys with her lips and it's nice to feel like we can actually be friends. "I can't believe you're letting me drive it. Do you know how much these things cost?"

I open my mouth to tell her money really isn't a big deal for me but quickly close it, remembering this is the same girl that didn't want to go out to grab a dinner with me because she didn't have the money for a proper meal.

I shrug and play it cool. "No clue, but I've got insurance. Besides, if you scratch it, I can find more creative ways for you to pay me back."

She rolls her eyes as she opens the driver's door. "If you want to make it through the next month with your nuts fully intact, I suggest you cut all your bullshit and quit trying to get in my pants."

I flop down in the passenger seat and glance over in her direction as she cranks the engine. As much as I know she's right—nothing can ever happen between us—it doesn't deter my normal, overly sexual personality. It's just the way I communicate with women. They always respond the way I want them to.

Well, they usually do.

Holly is an entirely new breed of woman for me. She doesn't give in easily to my bullshit lines, which is both frustrating and intriguing at the same time. It doesn't help that she's fucking beautiful, and I've tasted those perfect lips before.

I lean my head back against the headrest and allow my eyes to trace over every inch of her as she revs the motor and shifts gears. "You can drive stick. I'm impressed."

Holly's eyes cut towards me. "Why?"

"I guess it fits working on a track and all, but most hot girls can't do it. I think they're afraid they'll break a nail or some shit."

The tires bark as they meet the blacktop of the main stretch of road. "Not me. I love anything fast."

The bare skin showing on her thighs as her shorts ride up while she works the clutch is nearly enough to make me go out of my mind. They're so tanned and toned. I imagine her wrapping them around my waist and I have to restrain myself from biting my own knuckle and letting out a, "God damn".

Holly notices me staring at her as she slides her eyes towards me. "What are you looking at?"

I smirk as I think about telling her the truth and trying one more time to get in her pants, but then remember I love my balls far too much to push her much more. So, I do what any respectable guy caught in my position would do, lie. "Just wondering why someone like you doesn't have a boyfriend?"

Her brow furrows and her pretty pink lips twist. "Who says I don't have one?"

I chuckle. "No one has to tell me. It's obvious you don't."

Her heads whips to the right. "Yes … I mean no. Yes, someone had to tell you because no, it's not obvious."

I've flustered her. Maybe I can actually tap into what makes this girl tick. It would be nice to find common ground and make my relationship with her a little more pleasant. After all, if I have to deal with her indefinitely, I'd at least like us to be friendly.

I shrug. "I know you don't for two reasons. Number one, I've been with you most of the day and you haven't gotten one phone call or text from a guy." She opens her mouth to argue with me, but I cut her off. "Believe me, if I had a girl like you, I'd be calling all the time. And the second thing, no guy in their right mind would be okay letting his girl go anywhere with me. Women are defenseless against my sexiness. You should know that."

She laughs. "Oh. My. God. You are so full of yourself. I've never met anyone like you. If I hadn't been drunk last night, you wouldn't have got that far with me."

"Kid yourself all you want, sweetness. You liked it." I grin. "As for the comment about meeting anyone like me, I'll take it as a compliment."

"You shouldn't, because I didn't mean it as one."

"Well, however you meant it, I like standing out. You're talking to a guy who dyes his hair to do just that, remember?"

She smiles and nods. "Touché. Very true."

We ride in silence for a few more minutes and my mind drifts back to the topic of Holly and a boyfriend. I know she's kind of a bitch, or at least likes to come off as one, but I can't imagine one of these local yahoos couldn't overlook that to tap her fine ass on a regular basis. It's driving me nuts. "Really, I have to know. Why don't you have a boyfriend?"

She sighs. "I had one until recently, but he turned into kind of an asshole. So now I'm waiting until I find a guy who meets all the requirements on my checklist."

"Oh, God. You're not one of those crazy chicks that have a dream man in mind and turn away every decent guy that approaches you because he's not a doctor, lawyer or famous with lots of money are you?" Those kinds of women are the worst and a few of them have tried to get their hooks into me. I'll be damned if I ever let that happen.

"Absolutely not. I just want a real man that isn't a complete jackass and who appreciates me. I don't care about money and as far as fame is concerned, I would never date a famous person."

"What's wrong with famous people?"

"What's *not* wrong with them?" She lets out a sarcastic laugh. "They're egotistical, beautiful and they know it. Cheat on you any chance they get. You know, the real full of themselves types." She gives me a pointed look. "Kind of like you."

I don't know why, but my heart drops into my stomach. It's not like I'd ever date her, but hearing her confirm there'd be no way she'd date a celebrity like me is crushing.

I laugh nervously and do my best to throw her off my rock star scent. "Well, I can promise you that I'm just a regular guy. But I won't argue with you about me being beautiful. The ladies do love me, especially the cougars. They're all over this shit." I make a show of grabbing my junk.

"Eww. You are so gross," she mumbles.

I laugh at her salty reaction. "Don't knock it. There's something to be said about experience. I'm total cougar bait and I appreciate a woman who rides cock well."

She shakes her head. "You have no couth."

A deep laugh rumbles out of my chest. "*Couth?* Who uses that word anymore?

She shrugs. "I do. I don't see how you do it. Have sex with people like it means nothing, especially with someone who's a lot older than you. You know most of those kinds of relationships are just about sex, right? That's why I can't ever see myself dating an older man."

"What do you consider older?"

"Oh, I don't know, like ten years older than me."

"Do you think I'm too old for you?" I question.

Holly raises her right eyebrow and examines my face. "You can't be more than, what, twenty four? That's not too bad."

I clear my throat. "I'm twenty-five, actually."

"Really?"

"Why does that surprise you?"

"I don't know. I thought I was being generous with saying twenty-five. You act so much younger sometimes."

My lips pull into a tight line. "I should be deeply offended, but I'm not. I can be serious if I need to. Life's too short. I choose to have fun with it."

She nods. "I guess I can understand that philosophy."

Holly turns in to one of those chain steakhouses and asks if this place is okay. After I tell her it's fine, she whips into a parking spot and throws the manual transmission into neutral.

She grins as she revs the engine one last time before shutting it down. "I've never met a girl who's into cars before."

"That's because most girls are pampered princesses who don't understand the rush of going fast." She opens the car door and gets out, while I do the same.

I lean on the car and rest my arms on the roof to stare at her on the other side. "You're an adrenaline junkie?"

The twinkle in her blue eyes gives her away before she even admits it. "Totally."

I love anything that's fast and dangerous. It's what drew me to the motocross business. This hot little minx is kind of like the female version of me—apart from the fact she doesn't seem to be into casual sex. That's where we differ. "So, you ride on the track?"

"I used to." She nods towards the door of the restaurant we're parked in front of and we shut the car doors at the same time.

"Did you just get tired of it, or what?" I ask as I fall into step beside her.

"The passion for it isn't there anymore."

I hold the door open for her. "That doesn't make any sense. If you're so into the whole speed thing, I would think it's hard to walk away from riding if that's what you love. I mean, you're around it everyday. Don't you get the urge to hop on a bike and go?"

There's no answer from her, she only shrugs. She passes through the door and I can't help staring at her ass in those tight jean shorts. The temptation to smack it causes my hand to itch and I grip the door handle tighter.

The hostess wearing jeans and a purple t-shirts tosses her brown hair over her shoulder and smiles at me. "How many?"

I hold up two fingers. "Two."

The brunette gives Holly the once over and curls her lip. Holly doesn't miss the girl's reaction and raises her eyebrows, daring the girl to say something to her. The girl doesn't, she simply flips her hair again and says, "Follow me."

Holly turns towards me. "What a bitch. If we'd actually been together on a date, I would've been offended."

I can't help but to chuckle at the entire situation. "This can be a date if you want."

She shakes her head. "Um, no."

The hostess leads us to a corner booth and sets a couple of menus on the table. "Your server will be right with you." She turns her gaze to me and winks as I slide into the booth across from Holly. "Let me know if you need anything."

"Okay" —I lean in, staring at her nametag and perfectly round tits— "*Julie*. Will do."

I break out my crooked grin—the one that drives the ladies mad and return the wink. She giggles and plays with her hair as she spins on her heel to go back the direction she brought us.

"Ugh," Holly says. "Could you be any sleazier? You might as well have had sex with her right in front of me."

I laugh. "Are you jealous that you aren't getting my undivided flirting attention now? You've made it perfectly clear that you're not interested. Don't be a hater now that I'm testing new waters."

"Please." She rolls her eyes. "I don't care what you do."

She opens her menu upside-down and tries to ignore me, but I'm on to her. I reach across the table and flip it around. "For some who doesn't care, you're awfully distracted."

"Shut up." I laugh and pick up my menu and try to let it go before I piss her off any further.

This restaurant isn't fancy by any means—there are peanut shells thrown all over the floor—but it's nice. It's very country and reminds me of home.

I didn't see a lot of choices for places to eat when I drove through Tucson today. This city is so spread out. Not the typical packed city I'm used to, where it takes an hour to get anywhere, but I'm glad I have a local to show me around. It's been a while since I've had an adventure alone.

Holly studies the menu. "This place has the best Bloomin' Onions. Do you like those?"

I nod. "Sure, I just don't eat fried stuff often. This body is a temple. I try to keep it in shape."

She shakes her head. "I'd eat them every day if I could, but I can't afford to come here. Last time I was here was last fall for my nineteenth birthday when I came home from school."

"*Nineteen?* Wow you're a baby." And it's nearly illegal for me to have the dirty thoughts I've been having about her.

"Actually, last night was my birthday. That's why I was at the bar. I've officially left my teen years behind."

"Well, happy belated birthday. I'm glad I could give you a taste of being twenty." I smile and she scowls at me. "Maybe you should've let me give you a real present last night …" She shakes her head at me, but there's no hiding the blush in her cheeks.

I know deep down she likes it when I talk dirty to her. I can read people.

I need a subject change before I dwell on the things I'd like to do to her any longer. "You go to college?"

"I used to. I gave it up to come home and help Dad at the track. He couldn't afford to pay his employees anymore." I notice the frown on her lips, and I don't like it—a face that pretty should never be sad. I want to immediately fix it.

"Well, maybe when my investor buddy comes through you can go back?"

Her eyes flit to mine. "I would love to. It just sucks all my friends back at school will be ahead of me now."

"You're still young. You'll make new friends." I point out. "What were you studying?"

"Psychology."

My eyebrows shoot up. "Wow. That's impressive. You're smart *and* hot. That's a pretty badass combination."

She giggles. "Thanks. I wish more guys thought that way. A lot of them have problems with women who take school so seriously."

"What do you mean?" I ask completely confused. "I love smart women—all women, actually."

"I haven't had great luck with men."

That's a shame. I rest my elbows on the table and lean forward. "Maybe you've just been dating the wrong guys?"

There's a heat between us as we stare each other in the eye. I know she feels it too, because a slight blush creeps up her neck into her cheeks, making me think about what she'd look like after an orgasm. One that, at the moment, I would love to give her by sinking between her sweet, creamy thighs and licking her into oblivion.

Images of what's hidden beneath those clothes, and the way her mouth tastes, toy with my brain and my cock twitches in anticipation.

I open my mouth to tell her fuck the dinner—let's get out of here and I'll give her something else she's starving for when our overly chipper waitress with bottle-blonde hair approaches the table. "What can I get you two to drink?"

I shake myself out of my daze as I try to clear my sex-crazed brain from thinking about fucking Holly any longer. I can only endure so much torture. "A *Bud Light*."

"A *Coke*, please," Holly says.

Once the waitress is gone, Holly taps the table with her index finger and directs her attention at everyone else in the place but me. It's like she's afraid to look at me again. I completely get it—the attraction between us is hard to deny, but we both know we need to fight it.

There can never be anything more than innocent flirting between us and last night needs to be kept locked away.

It's a bad idea to mix business with pleasure. Even I know that.

Before I can start a conversation about the track, her eyes grown wide and she tries to hide her face behind her hands. "What are you doing, Holly? You look like a crazy person."

"Don't say my name," she whispers harshly, ducking down and grabbing for a menu.

"What? Why?" I turn around in my seat and notice a guy standing at the bar joking with the pretty, busty bartender. He's about my height, at least six foot, and is covered in tattoos, just like me. His head is shaved along with his face. She can't possibly be hiding from *that* guy. I turn back around and find Holly hiding behind the menu she picked up. "Why? Don't you want the guy at the bar to see you?"

"Yes. Please let me know when he's gone."

If I weren't so puzzled by this uncharacteristic deviation from the normal Ice Queen act I've seen from her so far, this would be hilarious. But my concern for her outweighs my personal amusement. What in the hell did that guy do to her? "Tell me who he is first."

She sighs dramatically and I bet if I could see her she'd be rolling her eyes. "He's Jackson Cruze." The tone in her voice makes it seem like it should be obvious to me who the guy is.

I glance up at the ceiling and try to go through my mental files on why that name sounds so familiar. It hits me. I do know that name. I saw it in one of the motocross magazines I read on the plane from Kentucky to here. I do a double-take of the guy and then ask her, "He's the *MX* hotshot, right? The one getting all the press right now?"

"Yes," she hisses.

I lean back in my seat. "Shouldn't you want to talk to a guy like that to get him to promote the track?"

She drops the menu and stares me in the eye. "No. He's the last person on earth I want to speak to."

I fold my arms on the table and lean in. "Why? I don't get it."

Holly's lips pull into a tight line. "He's my ex-boyfriend."

Light bulb. "Ah, I see. How recent?"

"Two weeks."

Ouch.

I nod. "I take it things didn't end on great terms?"

"No. He cheated on me. From what I've heard from the guys around the track who didn't say a word to me while we were together, he'd been sleeping around for a while. He made it into the pro-circuit while I was away at school last year, and I guess he's been with all the slutty, bimbos throwing themselves at him on a daily basis behind my back."

That's a story that hits a little too close to home and I find myself rolling my hands into fists in my lap. "Let me guess, you were blindsided when you caught him?"

She shakes her head. "He owned up to it after he forgot about the two-year anniversary date we were supposed to have."

I glance back and narrow my eyes at Jackson and say to Holly, "He sounds like an arrogant little shit stain that needs his ass beat."

Her soft lips twist like she's fighting back some tears. "Maybe so, but I even after everything he did to me, I don't wish him any physical harm."

I know I haven't known Holly very long, and it's insane to feel protective over her, but I know exactly what she's going through. Being cheated on sucks, especially when the person you love blindsides you.

How dare that douchebag do that to this beautiful, caring girl who obviously loves him. She's a fucking prize, and if that little twerp couldn't see that, he didn't deserve her anyway.

"Oh, God. He's coming over here. Ignore him," she orders.

I open my mouth to protest, but Jackson stops at our table. "Holly? How are you?"

Holly stares up at him and smiles. "Hi, Jackson. I'm fine."

His eyes drift down her body and linger awhile on her tits beneath her white tank-top. "You look great."

What he means to say is that her tits look great—which they do—but after the way he treated her she shouldn't give him the satisfaction of looking at them. She should tell him to piss off, but she doesn't. She actually bats her eyes at him and as she tells him he looks good too.

I don't fucking get chicks. At. All.

This asshole did her wrong. Why is she being nice to him? One minute she hates him, and the next he has her under some sort of fucked up spell that's turned the baddest chick I know into, well … she's acting just like the shallow groupies who try to get my attention. Why would she even want him back after what he did?

This isn't good. Doesn't she know with this groupie act she'll be just another easy mark for him? He'll have the same thing on his mind that I normally do when it comes to women—fuck 'em and dump 'em—and Holly is too good for that. She's not some random bimbo out for a good time. I've been around her long enough today to know she's loyal and fierce, and deserves so much more.

I'm going to make sure that happens.

I reach across the table and intertwine my fingers with hers. "Who's this, baby?"

Holly attempts to pull away, but I squeeze my fingers together, holding her in place. The little touch works. Jackson's brown eyes zero in on it, and I smirk at Holly.

It takes her a couple seconds to realize that I'm helping her out and she smiles at me. "This is my friend, Jackson."

I let go of her hand and stand up from the booth and extend my hand. "What's up, man. I'm Trip."

Jackson sizes me up, glancing down at my biceps before allowing a smirk to fill his face. He's confident, and thinks he's better than even me. If he's not careful, I'll wipe that smart-ass grin off his face for him. "I thought I knew all of Holly's friends?"

I continue shaking his hand, squeezing a little tighter. "I've known her for a little while now—she's really something." I look down at her and wink.

Jackson lets go of my hand, and flexes his fingers. This time it's my turn to wear a shit-eating grin.

He turns to Holly. "I know we aren't on the best terms right now, but I'd love to stop out at the track. Would that be okay?"

Her face lights up. "Of course! We'd love to have you there."

"Great. It's a date. I'll be there tomorrow," Jackson answers with a grin before he turns back to me. "Nice to meet you, Trip. I'm sure I'll see you around."

I nod. "You can count on it."

I take my seat and shake my head as Holly watches Jackson walk out the door. "What do you see in him?"

She turns back to me. "I don't see anything in him."

I roll my eyes. "Give me a break. If I hadn't saved your ass, you would've been a pile of girl-goo all over the floor. If you want to make a guy like him jealous, you have to be a challenge. You can't go around throwing yourself at him."

"I wasn't throwing myself at him."

I point at the table. "Yeah, you were. Trust me. I know what I'm talking about. You want this guy to notice you and kick himself for letting you go, you're going to need my help. You have to make him come crawling back. He needs to suffer for doing you wrong, so he'll know not to ever do it again."

She crosses her arms. "Why would you even offer that? I've been a royal bitch to you for the most part. What's in it for you?"

I shrug. "I want my time here to go as smoothly as possible. I'd like us to be friends as well as co-workers. I feel like shit for how I treated you at the club and I'm hoping this will get me on your good side. Your friendship will make my job fun. This little pact will provide my entertainment while I'm here and you'll be getting something in return. I'd say that's a win-win."

She toys with a strand of her blonde hair. "So, you're saying if we form this un-holy alliance, the only thing I have to do is be nice to you? There's nothing else you want in return from me?"

I shake my head. "Nothing else. I promise. I only want your friendship and the chance to help you make a cheater pay. I have no love for cheaters. I know first hand how many fucking problems cheating in a relationship can cause."

Holly narrows her blue eyes. "You'll behave?"

"Yes. I promise I'll keep my dick in my pants when it comes to you. I'm starting to like you too much to fuck you, anyhow." I tell her the honest truth, because I know now she's the relationship type, and that's not what I'm here for. I don't want to pretend like I'd be into one with her because I won't allow myself to play her just to have sex. I won't be able to toss her aside like I do the rest. I already like her to much to do that.

"That makes no sense. You like me too much now to sleep with me? That's just an odd thing to say, but whatever. The deal seems pretty simple, and I would love to give Jackson a taste of his own medicine and make his ass jealous. It'd be nice to prove to him I can find someone else too."

"The way I see it, Holly, if my buddy goes into business with your dad, we'll see a lot of each other. I would like us to be on good terms. I'll probably be around from time to time after my month here is over and I'd like to walk into your office and have you greet me with a smile instead of a scowl. You're far to pretty to have an ugly expression on that beautiful face."

She bites her bottom lip. "I completely get what you're saying. I don't want a bad relationship with you either. I think teaming up with you could be fun, but no more flirting with me."

I shake my head. "Jackson believes we're together, so we're going to have to play the part. There will be flirting—lots of it. It's the only way this will be believable."

She leans back in the booth and chews her thumbnail while she weighs up her options.

"Clock's ticking," I say. "You better make up your mind. He's coming to see you tomorrow. You can either allow me to fondle you in front of Jackson, making him insanely jealous, or you can go back to hating my guts. The choice is yours."

Her eyes soften. "I never said I hated you."

"Actions speak louder than words, sweetness. You haven't had many kind things to say to me today." I extend my hand across the table to her. "What do you say? Do we have a deal?"

She leans forward and places her hand in mine. "Deal. And I promise I'll start being nicer."

Looks like my time here just got a hell of a lot more enjoyable. I smile and give her hand a shake. This looks like the beginning of a beautiful friendship.

Chapter Five

"I Wanna Be Bad"

Holly

What the hell did I agree to? That's the only thought that keeps flitting through my mind as I stare straight ahead on our car ride back to the house. This little game is dangerous. Trip is dangerous. I know that. Every sense in my body screams it. It's worrisome that I've agree to act like Trip and I are an item, considering I know that I'm attracted to him physically, but what he was offering was too sweet of a deal to turn down. Jackson needs to see that I can move on and that my life doesn't revolve around him. I can't let him know he nearly broke me.

When I was seventeen, Jackson Cruze was my everything. Even now, it's a hard to pretend I don't feel something for him. I've drooled over him since I was old enough to like boys in the first place. The moment he came to my father's track and flashed his dimples at me I was a goner. Jackson was my first real crush, my first boyfriend, and the first guy I ever fell in love with—that all means something to me. What he did to me doesn't instantly erase all that, although I wish it would. As much as I hate it, I want him back.

Trips downshifts the Mustang as we round the corner and slow down. He pulls into the drive leading to the office and our house. "Where should I park?"

I point to our house. "You can pull up there since you're staying with us."

His eyes slide in my direction. "That'll help you know."

"What?"

"Me living with you. It'll drive Jackson nuts knowing we're probably sleeping together every night."

I shake my head. "I think you're wrong about him. He won't be that jealous over me. He left me, remember?"

He cuts the ignition and sets his gaze on me. "He wants you. He wouldn't have attempted to push my buttons by making a *date* with you in front of me if he wasn't. Jackson wants me to know I'm treading in his territory."

"Jeesh, you make it sound like it's a pissing contest."

"In a manner of speaking, it is. In his eyes, the man that fights for you the hardest will win. We just have to see how far he's willing to take this."

"What if he doesn't?" I drop my head down, hating the thought of being rejected by Jackson yet again.

Trip softly pinches my chin and forces me to look into his eyes. "He will. You're worth fighting for. Any idiot can see that. Now that he sees you've moved on so easily He knows he was a fool for ever letting you go. It's his turn to feel the sting of rejection. Trust me, he wants you back."

My mouth drifts open and I stare at Trip's inviting lips. He's not at all like I expected. When I first laid eyes on him, I wanted him. But after I saw how our kiss meant nothing to him, I assumed he was just another lame asshole who only cared about getting some ass. This side of him though, is caring and helpful. It makes him even more appealing, which is a very bad thing. It's wrong to want him, especially considering he's helping me win back the affection of another man.

His eyes search my face, before he ultimately decides to release me. "It's getting late. We'd better go inside so I can unpack and get a good night's rest. We've got an old boyfriend jealous tomorrow, remember?"

I swallow hard and nod in agreement still looking into his eyes. "Sleeping with you would be good." He laughs and I quickly throw my hand over my mouth. I immediately try to correct my mistake. "I mean, sleeping would be good." This only makes him laugh harder and I let out a frustrated breath. "Stop. You know what I meant."

I want to shove my head in a pile of desert sand.

"I think it was a subconscious slip," he says, adjusting his hat and winking at me before he opens his door to get out.

I trail behind him after I shut the car door behind me. "It was not."

He steps up onto the porch and leans against the house right by the door. I feel his heated gaze on me while I fish the keys from my pocket. "Keep telling yourself that, sweetness. It's okay to admit you'd like to fuck me, because I think it's pretty clear I'd like the same thing. It's too bad we can't now that we're co-workers and co-conspirators. I'm pretty sure that'd be bad for business."

"Shhhh," I scold him. "My dad might hear you." I growl when the second key I try in the lock doesn't work. "Come on."

Trip leans down and whispers in my ear, "I know just the thing to relieve that tension."

I lift my shoulder, trying to shove him out of my ear as I allow the door to fly open. "Yes."

He chuckles as he follows me inside. "That was pretty

enthusiastic. I can only imagine what that would sound like when you're—"

The lights flip on in the foyer and Trip quickly closes his mouth, while my cheeks burn even hotter. No one wants their parents to hear a conversation like that.

Dad tightens his paper-thin blue robe around his small waist and glances up at the clock above our heads. "I wondered when you two would get back. Dinner's in the refrigerator if you're hungry."

Guilt pours over me. "Sorry, Dad. I should've check with you before I agreed to go out to eat with Trip. We should've invited you."

He rubs his eyes. "It's okay. I was really tired anyhow. Well, now that I know you're home safe, I'm heading back to bed."

"Are you still feeling sick?" I ask, completely concerned.

His weight-loss and coupled with how exhausted he's felt lately has me a bit worried. Dad's always on the go. The idea that he's in bed so early, so often, is odd for him. He typically has more energy than I do.

He nods. "A little. I hope a few more days of hitting the sack early will perk me up out of this funk I've been fighting these last couple of months."

"I think it's time you make a doctor's appointment. You've felt like this for way too long." We've been over this before, and I hate to push the subject, but I'm worried.

"I can't, Holly. They'll want to do all sorts of tests we can't afford. If it gets too bad, I'll go. I promise." Dad offers a small hint of a smile. "Well, goodnight, kids. I'll see you both down at the office bright and early. Trip, we'll get you out on the track tomorrow so you can check it."

Trip nods and smiles. "Sounds good."

Dad turns and shuts himself back in his bedroom and I stare at the door. Whatever is going on with him, I don't like it.

I turn towards Trip. "Do you have bags in your car that need to be carried up?"

"I have a duffel bag."

"That's it for an entire month?"

He shrugs. "I'm used to being on the road a lot. Packing light becomes second nature when you get tired of carrying around a ton of shit. Besides, I figured wherever I stayed would have a washer and dryer. It's not like I'll run around like a homeless bum."

That makes me curious about him and his money-bags boss. Is he looking at another track, too? Do we have competition on this deal? "You check out a lot of tracks for this investor?"

"This is the first one, actually."

I raise an eyebrow. "So, what else do you check out for him? I know cattle farmers can't possibly travel that much. Who would feed the livestock?"

Trip scratches the back of his head, almost like he's nervous and it takes him a while to answer me. "I'm not actually a cow farmer."

I smile. "I never believed for a second you were. What is it that you actually do?"

"I'm a personal assistant to a musician." His answer is simple and makes much more sense. I'd never seen a farmer who looked like him before. A biker? Yes. A guy in a rock band? Yes. A farmer? No.

Since he's opening up to me, I wonder if I can get him to spill the secret of the investor's identity. "Now that, I believe. So tell me, is this investor a musician?"

Trip shakes his head and takes a step backwards to the door. "I'll never tell."

"Come on. I just want to know who is interested, that's all. I can keep a secret. I swear." Even I can hear the little whine in my voice, but knowing who might become out partner in the business is vital. If it's the right person, we can use their celebrity status to draw in bigger events.

His hand rests on the doorknob. "Sorry, sweetness. I can't give you that information. It'll ruin everything."

"Will we ever find out?" I question.

Trip opens the door and glances up at me with a smile on his lips. "You will, when the time is right."

"Can I at least have a hint?"

He tilts his head. "Let's call him Mr. Snare."

My eyes widen as the last name clicks. "He's a drummer?"

He shoots me a cocky grin that almost makes me weak in the knees. "Maybe."

Before I get a chance to ask any more questions he slips out the door.

I turn and grab the handrail as I walk slowly up the stairs trying to pinpoint what drummer could possibly be the investor. Dad's friend at the bank told him he didn't have much information either, only that the person investing wanted to remain undisclosed until Trip thoroughly investigates the place and reports back to him. If the person investing is some rock star that could be great for business. It can kind of be what *Carey Hart* did for the tattoo business in Las Vegas. His name alone draws people to that shop he owns there.

This is excellent news.

I shut myself in my room and grab my laptop off the nightstand. Surely I'll be able to find something.

I enter drummer into the search field and wait on the results. I groan. Over five million results pop up. "This is ridiculous. It's like trying to find a needle in a haystack."

I push the screen down before I place it away. There's no way I can ever figure out who it is by going through that mess.

I lay back, falling into stack of pillows behind me on my full size bed. My finger traces patterns on the blue bedspread as I allow my mind to wander at what the future for this place may hold. I close my eyes and try to picture the bands I know. Not many individual members of bands come to mind. When I think of a band, I think of them as a whole. I've never really had the desire to study individual members of a band. I can't even name five drummers.

I don't even know where to start. Trip didn't say if it's a new band, or a retired one or what. The chances of me figuring this out on my own aren't very good. I could try looking up Trip, but unless he's got a website, which I doubt, linking him with the band, that probably won't be very helpful. It would be a further waste of my time.

I'm going to have to get him to tell me himself.

The image of Trip smiling as he backed out of the door pops in my head. He's dangerously sexy. His smile alone is hot enough to nearly melt my panties right off my body.

For the past couple years, Jackson has been the only man I've thought of, so it's hard to tell my brain that it's okay to move on and find other men attractive. Take Trip for example—as much as I hate to admit it to myself, Trip is exactly my type of guy. He's cocky, sexy, and yet still has an excellent sense of humor. I can't believe he's willing to help me make Jackson jealous. It's sweet and he couldn't possibly understand how much that means to me.

It sucked to find out that all the years we spent together meant nothing to Jackson—that he thought so little of me that he could throw me out like a piece of candy that had lost its flavor. It changes everything when you find out what you thought was real is a lie. I am hurt and I'll admit that I want to hurt him back.

If Trip is right, and the sight of the two of us together bothers

Jackson, it'll be the best payback I can ask for.

At some point while all that was running through my head I must've fallen asleep because the next thing I know a steady stream of sunlight pours through the window, hitting me in the eyes.

Shit. I'm late. The regular riders like an early start when they come to ride on open track day.

I throw my hand over my face to shield myself from the glare as I sit up and gain my bearings. I place both feet on the hardwood floor below me and push myself off the bed, tugging my nightshirt down around my thighs on my way to the bathroom.

I yawn as I open the door to answer nature's morning call. My yawn quickly turns into a sucked-in breath as my wide eyes land on a tanned, toned, and *very* naked Trip, standing at the bathroom counter, brushing his teeth. My eyes zero in on his mid-section, and promptly widen. Oh. My. God! His dick is right there on display for the world to see. Okay, maybe not the world, but I certainly have an eyeful.

Quickly, I turn my head to keep myself from staring any longer as heat creeps up my neck before settling in my cheeks. "What are you doing?!"

"What's it look like I'm doing? I'm brushing my teeth. Oral hygiene is very important," he says with his mouth full.

I sigh but it almost sounds like a growl. "I meant *why* are you naked?"

"Um, you're supposed to be naked in the shower." I don't even have to see his face to know he's smiling and having a good time with this.

I grab a white towel off the rod on the wall and thrust it in his direction. "Here. Cover that *thing* up."

He spits in the sink and then his deep laugh fills the tiny bathroom as he takes the towel. "*Thing?* What are we in fifth grade? It's a cock,

Holly. Call it what it is."

I peek out the corner of my eye and Trip flings the towel over his shoulder, turning so I can get a full view of his mouth-watering naked form. "That was to go around your waist."

He leans causally against the counter. Obviously he's not a bit shy about being completely naked in front of me. "Look, men want women who aren't afraid to talk dirty. This can be our first lesson in how to catch a guy's interest. If you want me to cover up, quit being a scared little virgin, and grab my attention. Look me in the eye and tell me to cover my cock."

I roll my eyes. "This is ridiculous."

"You want my help or not?" When I don't answer right away, he drums his fingers on the counter. "I'm waiting … I can stand here like this all day. I have no problem showing off what God blessed me with, and when I say blessed, well, you know. You've seen it." He chuckles.

My lips pull into a tight line. As much as I hate the idea of sinking to this embarrassing level with him, I know deep down he's right. I've always heard men like their women to be the sinner and the saint. I need to suck it up and do this. I want to prove to Jackson and everyone else that there's more to me than just this straight-laced good girl that they all think I am.

His green eyes burn into mine the moment our gaze meets. "Cover your fucking cock, you dirty manwhore."

He smirks and pulls the towel off his shoulder slowly with one hand. The tattoos etched into the smooth skin of his arms, shoulders and chest catch my eye as Trip wraps the towel around his waist. "There may be hope for you after all, sweetness. We've still got a lot of work to do, though. We've got to keep working on making that pretty little mouth of yours dirty."

I fold my arms over my chest. "Fine. We will. Now, can you

please get out so I can pee?"

"Sure thing." Trip winks at me before squeezing past me, slapping my ass on his way out.

My skin burns from his touch, and I rub my backside to console it. "Hey!"

"Just warming that booty up for later. Get used to my touch, babe." He holds his hands up and makes a grabbing motion with his hands while his back stays to me. "These things are going to be all over you today."

"Ugh." I close the door a little harder than I mean to in order to get away from him. No matter what, I have to remind myself it's important to be nice to Trip. He's helping me with the two most important things in my life: this track, and getting back with Jackson.

I stare at myself in the mirror and study my reflection as I curse myself for allowing him to get to me. I need to learn to let things go and stop getting riled up so quickly.

I toss my hair over my shoulder and turn on the water. My blue eyes stare back at me as I wait for the water to warm up. The vision of Trip smiling and flexing his fingers as he talks about groping me floats through my mind. I wish the thought of his strong hands being all over me didn't make my stomach flutter the way it's doing right now. Damn him.

I throw some water on my face and glance back at the clock on the wall behind me. It's not as late as I thought. I've got time for my normal routine. I pull my shirt over my head and take off my underwear in order to grab a quick shower. I slide the shower curtain back and turn on the water just as the bathroom door flings open.

I yank the shower curtain over my naked body and stagger at the same moment I pivot.

Trip's large hand grabs my elbow to steady me. "You all right there?"

I jerk away from him. I don't like the idea of him touching me while I'm completely naked. "Don't you knock?"

"You didn't, so I figured our relationship had already progressed to the 'no knocking' level."

I shove his shoulder towards the open door, careful to keep the plastic wrapped around me. "Well it hasn't, now get out."

He holds up his hands. "Easy. I just came for my toothbrush and deodorant. I promise I won't peek, unless you want me to."

"Get out," I order.

"Say please." I narrow my eyes at him and he raises his eyebrow. "Our deal …"

This is literally killing me. "Ugh. Fine. Please, get out."

He grabs his stuff off the counter and grins. "Only because you begged. I can't ever turn a woman down when she begs me to do something for her."

I fight the urge to scream at him, and tell him I've changed my mind and our deal isn't worth it when he laughs at me yet again. I want to, but I won't. I need to see this thing through. I'm tired of thinking about Jackson all the time. Even I know it's pathetic, this little deal with Trip will help me see these feelings I've been harboring through. Jackson will either want me back, or he'll continue to pretend that what we had was nothing—which will tell me it's really over.

Either way, I'm ready to move on with my life. I need a new direction, and I want to find someone who actually wants me.

Chapter Six

"Love Crime"

Trip

I walk towards the office my cell vibrates and I yank it out of my pocket. I check the caller ID and roll my eyes. "Yes, *Dad?*"

"Well maybe if you would check in from time to time and let people know where you are, I wouldn't be checking up on you. Where are you?" my twin brother, Tyke, asks, enough angst in his voice to create the next teen blockbuster.

I slip my sunglasses on and glance around at the mountain scenery. "I'm in Arizona."

"What the fuck for?"

Having a brother so involved in your life is a pain in the ass sometimes. "Charlie Richardson, our financial investor, called with a killer investment opportunity and I had to jump on it right away. So, that's what I'm doing … checking shit out."

Tyke sighs into the phone. "And you didn't think to call me and let me know. Jesus, man, I've been fucking worried about your stupid ass. It isn't like you to take off for days and not let me know where you are. Why didn't you call me back? I left you, like, fifteen messages."

"I don't have to tell you everything," I argue.

"I know, but, damn. A little common courtesy would be nice. I thought one of our psycho fans finally lost their mind and had you tied to their bed somewhere like *Misery*."

I laugh. "That might not necessarily be a bad thing. The groupies I bang are always smokin' hot. A few days being someone's sex slave could be kind of fun."

"Trip …" My brother is a fucking worrywart. Most of the time he's too serious for his own good, and it gets on my nerves. "I'm just asking next time you let me know. Anna was worried too."

You would think Anna, our housekeeper, is my mother the way she frets over Tyke and I. "Yeah, okay. I'm sorry. This all happened so fast, I didn't even cross my mind to tell you I was leaving. And I know it's not a very good excuse, but I've been really busy from the moment I got here. Calling you slipped my mind. Tell Anna I'm sorry."

"I will. So, tell me—what's this business that's got you so pumped, and how long are you going to be gone?"

"A motocross track, and I'll be back in a few weeks. I need to stick around here and get a good feel for the place."

"You know those are money-pits, right?"

I shake my head even though he can't see me. "Not if the place has the right sponsors and they hold big events. There's money to be made. Besides, you know how I like off the wall shit. This place is the perfect business for me."

"But, Trip, this isn't like buying a personal playground. It's going to affect other people when you make a bad decision."

"Are you saying I can't handle running something like this?"

"No, with help, I'm sure you'll be fine. What I *am* saying is that I know you. When you set your sights on something, you don't stop until you get it—even if it's not for the best. You aren't very restrained."

Shows how much he knows. I want Holly and I've showed nothing but restraint since I figured out who she is. I think that proves I can do anything to make this business work. I've pushed my own sexual desires to possess her out of the way in order to make this right. "That's where you're wrong, Tyke. I know I can do this."

"How much are you buying the track for?"

I kick at the gravel with my toe. "I'm not buying it, exactly. It's more like a bail-out loan, then I become a silent partner."

"That sounds more your speed. Taking on a business is a lot of work."

"I know that. I'm not a complete idiot. I know I can't run something entirely by myself."

"No one ever said you were. I think this is a smart move actually."

I scratch the back of my neck. "You do?"

"Yeah. This band may not last forever."

I raise my eyebrows. He's never said anything like that before. It's not like him. Tyke loves Black Falcon just as much as I do. "Why would you say that?"

He sighs into the phone. "Forget I said anything. I'm just talking crazy."

"Am I missing something? Did Noel or Riff say something about the band breaking up?" I can hear the near panic on my own voice.

"No. I'm just saying we're all starting to go in different directions, is all."

"We are not. Everyone just needs a break. Once Noel and Riff get their fill of the chicks they're with, it'll all be out of their systems and things will get back to normal."

"I hope so. Haven't you noticed we hardly see them anymore?"

"Damn, dude, stop being so harsh. Give them time before you

doubt them. They'll bounce back. You'll see."

"I hope you're right, baby brother."

"Aren't I always right? And stop calling me that. Who cares that you're five minutes older. Big fucking whoop."

Tyke laughs. "Obviously you do."

"Whatever, man. I'll call you later."

"All right. Don't forget to come up with beats for the new songs we were working on before you took off."

"Will do," is all I say before ending the call.

I shove my phone back in my pocket and continue across the gravel lot to the shop. When I step onto the porch I spot Holly through the window and I smile. The thoughts I've been having about how fucking fantastic she would look naked were confirmed this morning when I walked in on her in nothing but that tight, little birthday suit. I wonder if she's thought about me since the other night in the bar. I didn't leave anything to the imagination this morning when I gave her the full Trip show in the bathroom, so I bet she's thinking about me now.

My morning was made when I heard that pretty mouth of hers say "cock". I won't lie and say that wasn't fucking hot because it totally was. I can practically picture her on her knees begging to wrap her lips around my cock. My pants fit a little snugger as the image becomes clearer.

What the fuck am I doing? Damn it. Think of something else. I start counting off a beat like I do at our shows and then start humming *Ball Busting Bitch* as I open the door.

Holly's gaze whips in my direction. "I've heard that song before."

I instantly stop singing and raise an eyebrow. "Oh yeah? You like it?"

She shakes her head. "Not my kind of music. Besides, it got

completely played out."

I have to stop myself from busting out in a fit of laughter. If she only knew how sick of that song I am myself. Playing it nearly every damn day of my life gets a little old.

Finally, I grin at her and wink. "I know exactly what you mean."

She quickly looks away and goes back to counting the money for her drawer. Her hair is loose today, falling over her shoulders in waves and her make-up is a little heavier than yesterday, reminding me of when I first spotted her in the nightclub. Even with that stupid gray uniform top—which makes her look more like a mechanic than anything else—she's hot. There's no fucking denying it.

She writes down the total when she's done counting and she puts the pen in her mouth, effectively wrapping her soft lips around it, bringing back the vision of her blowing me. I know the simple gesture she's doing with the pen isn't sexual in any way, but try telling my fucking dick that. The motherfucker is twitching in my pants at the very sight of it.

Damn. Down, boy.

Holly glances up and catches me staring at her. "What?"

I pull her hand with the pen away from her mouth. "No distracting the teacher."

Her eyes flit to the pen. "I don't get it."

"Men get distracted when a woman puts things in her mouth, especially when we imagine it's our dick you're sucking on," I answer honestly. "If I'm going teach you how to hook a guy, then you need to know how we think."

She rolls her eyes. "Not all guys are like that."

"If it walks with a dick, and thinks with a dick … it's a guy. Trust me on this. I am one, and I know how we operate. Sex rules us."

Her lips twitch like she's ready to laugh at me. "All right fine, oh wise one. Teach me."

I walk around her, enjoying the free roam she is allowing my appraising eyes. This is going to be fun.

Holly

Trip pulls on the tops of my arms from behind me. "Put your shoulders back more when you stand."

"This feels awkward."

"It probably does, but men notice tits, and you've got an excellent set. Use them to your advantage." He walks around assessing me. "There's not much we can do with the uniform since Bill is so stuck on you wearing it, but we can figure out other ways to show off that hot body of yours."

Surely there's more to like about me other than that. "Jackson isn't that shallow."

Trip raises his eyebrow. "You're talking about the same guy that left you to go after looser pieces of ass. Trust me, he's a guy—we're all shallow. Whatever you guys had before is over. We're starting from scratch."

I laugh. "At least you're honest. It's sort of refreshing."

He shrugs his thick shoulders. "There's no other way to be. Now, let's work on flirting."

I grin. "Oh, I can flirt, so we can skip that. I've already got that down."

He fights back a smile. "Really?"

I throw my hands on my hips. "It worked on you at the club didn't it?"

He steps in front of me and his eyes zero in on my chest. Both of his hands dart to my top button on my gray top and he releases it from its hole before moving on to the next one. "First of all, I was attracted to your banging body in that little black dress. It screamed, "Fuck me," so that's not flirting—that's attention seeking. Believe me, I wasn't the only one watching you shake your ass. I was just the only one brave enough to try and get with you even though you were there with another man."

"You thought I was there with Max?" I ask even though it doesn't surprise me. Max isn't exactly the stereotypically homosexual male. There's nothing feminine about him. People make the mistake that we're an item all the time.

"Yep."

"And you were what, going to steal me away from my date?"

Trip shrugs. "When I see something I want, I go after it. And that night I wanted you. That is until you let him drag you away from me. I figured it wasn't worth the scene it would cause to kick his ass."

I roll my eyes. "How do you know you wouldn't have been the one on the receiving end of that ass-kicking? Max is a pretty strong dude."

He gives me a pointed look. "If there's one thing I know besides that I'm awesome in bed, is that I can fight."

I sigh. "Okay, so you're a badass—I get it. What's the other reason you think I can't flirt?"

He smiles. "I win the flirting debate because I believe it was me who came on to you first, so you can't take credit for that."

My brain attempts to wade through the drunken memories of a

couple nights ago. "You may have started the dance, but I believe I'm the one who turned around to take it to that next level, allowing you to kiss me. Therefore I finished it. I get total credit for flirting with you first."

He undoes the last button on my shirt. "No. Max dragged you away, effectively cutting us both off for the night. And Thank God for that. He deserves a fucking medal for performing a good deed. Can you imagine how awkward all this would be if we'd had crazy sex that night, only to meet up the very next day? That would've been a nightmare."

I flinch. "Am I really that horrible that you would've regretted sleeping with me?"

Am I really that big of a bitch that people actually find me repulsive?

Trip tilts his head and slides his index finger under my chin. "You really have no clue how beautiful you are, do you?" When I shake my head, he takes a deep breath and then licks his lips. "Since you are oblivious as to what men see when they look at you I'm going to be blunt. I know myself well enough to know if I would've gotten a taste of that sweet little pussy of yours, I would have a full-on addiction. I could never maintain a purely professional relationship with you if that ever happens. I've tasted your lips, and that alone has me constantly thinking about you. I can't even begin to image what being buried deep inside you would do to me."

My eyes widen. No one has ever spoken to me like that before. It's so dirty and primal, and … *sexy*. I ball my hands into tight fists at my side to keep them from reaching out to cling to him, but he's right. Even if we find each other attractive, we can never act on it. It would ruin everything. His job, my family's business, not to mention any chance I have of getting Jackson back—that would all be in danger. "You shouldn't say things like that to people."

Trip gazes into my eyes. "Why shouldn't I? It's the truth. Don't tell me you haven't thought about that night. What it would've been like if Max hadn't stopped us."

Heat pools in my belly and all I can think about is tasting his mouth, and how much I want to do it again.

Gah! What in the hell am I thinking? I shouldn't want that. I can't want that. I want Jackson, right? He's the guy I'm supposed to be with. Isn't the guy you've known your entire life the safer bet? Max's words about Trip being a tasty piece of danger ring in my mind. He is so right. Trip is dangerous, and tasty, and I do need to stay away from him. He makes me want things I shouldn't with a guy I know isn't going to be sticking around much longer.

Trip is a heartbreaker. I saw with my own eyes how easily he can move on to someone else. I know I get too attached when it comes to men. It might've been different if I never saw him again after a one-night stand, but now I know him, which only further confirms we can never be together.

As I stare into Trip's eyes, I can see him struggling too. Even through all the outrageous flirting, I can tell he's been trying to keep his distance and behave.

I take a step back and clear my throat, trying to rid us of the strange, sexual tension in the air. "Okay, what next?"

He shakes his head like he's coming out of a daze. "Since you know flirting, let's skip to the biggest flirt of them all. Give me your best fuck-eye."

My lips pull into a tight line because I'm clueless as what he wants me to do. "My *what?*"

He folds his arms across his chest. "You know the look that says, "Hey, I wanna fuck your brains out."

My lips twist and I start to make the most sensual face I can, but I can tell by the laugh he's holding back that I look more like a dying duck than a sexy woman. "I suck at this. Let's move on."

Trip chuckles. "No. If you want a man to notice you, it's important to nail the *come hither* look. It gives people the guts to approach if they know they won't be rejected. Here, like this."

He tips his head down and then lifts his chin, effectively giving me the smoldering look that the fictional, cartoon character gives in that one movie. I have to admit, it's pretty damn good. There's no doubt what that look means. It's quite impressive he can turn it on so quickly.

"Trip …" I begin to tell him there's no way I can do that.

"Shut up. I'm eye-fucking you. Don't break my concentration," he says without changing his expression.

I shake my head. "Well, not everyone is as good as you at that. We can't all be sluts."

The sexy look morphs into a concerned one. "Who said I was a slut?"

I roll my eyes. "Please. I saw how fast you rebounded from me at the club."

One side of his mouth pulls down. "You caught that, huh?"

"Yeah, I did."

He leans into me. "Just so you know, she was a lousy lay. I imagine you would've been a thousand times more fun."

"Jeesh, thanks. That's supposed to make me feel better?"

"It would me. I'd be a happy man to know you like to think of me while getting pleasured."

I shake my head. "You and that mouth."

"What?" he laughs.

"Well, it's dangerous. Max was right about you."

"You and Max talk about me, huh?"

I shrug. "A little."

"Girl talk?"

He eyes snap in my direction. "What do you mean by that?"

"Come on. It's not like it's a huge secret that he's gay."

I narrow my eyes. "It is around here. How did you know?"

I quickly think back, and there's not one moment I can recall where I may have disclosed Max's secret.

"It was an easy guess. When he acted all put-off when I asked if he was your man, I knew right then he was probably gay. No guy in his right, heterosexual mind would be turned off when thinking about tapping what's between your legs."

I know in his twisted brain that was probably a compliment, but his vulgarity won out, making it a feel a little sleazy. "Thanks ... I think. Max is my best friend, and I guess if we are pretending to date, you should know that."

Trip nods. "You're right. We should really get to know each other to make this feel real. What else can you tell me?"

I bite the inside corner of my lower lip. "There's not much to know, really."

"How about sexual history. Couples usually talk about that pretty early on in a relationship. If Jackson says something to me about it, I want to be prepared."

My stomach squeezes for a brief second like we've just hit the first big drop on a roller coaster. I hate the idea of Trip knowing I've only slept with one man my entire life, and it just happens to be the one guy I'm trying to win back. I'm sure it'll give him a good laugh, knowing I'm such a prude. He'll never let me live it down. But in order for us to make this lie work, I should at least be honest with him. "Only one."

There's a look of surprise on his face. "Really? Wow."

"Why would that surprise you?" I'm a little offended he would believe for a second I'm an easy lay.

"At the club, the way you moved, that said to me you had volumes of experience."

Whatever. That's like judging a book from its drunken cover. "Just because a girl dances a certain way doesn't mean she's been around a lot."

"You're right. I shouldn't be so quick to tramp-stamp a girl, but you have to admit, the way you moved that night wasn't virginal."

I fold my arms. "Just because I said I've only been with one person doesn't mean I'm not experienced."

Trip reaches out and runs his fingers down the bare skin on my arms. "Believe me, sweetness, you're inexperienced until you've been with me. If I fucked you, I'd take you to a whole other level."

My mouth drifts open and I squeeze my thighs together, trying to relieve the tingle between my legs. The way those naughty words roll off his tongue makes me wonder what other wicked things it can do.

Trip's gaze holds mine. It's like he's waiting for permission to pounce on me. I think I want this. I've been thinking more about him today than I have Jackson. All his teasing is driving me crazy.

I open my mouth to drive deeper into the subject of us having some crazy-random sex together, the screen door shuts, jerking me attention away from Trip. "I'm not interrupting anything, am I?"

Jackson Cruze stands in my doorway with his black and white riding gear on and smiles a smile so beautiful it makes me nearly forget the heat I was feeling with Trip only moments ago. I pull my arm away from Trip's touch and shake my head. "No. Come on in. I'm glad you came."

"Me too," Jackson says as I step around the counter and allow his eyes to roam over my body. Remembering Trip's coaching, I allow my shoulders to fall back and arch my back a bit. It totally works as I catch Jackson's hungry eyes inspecting my breasts beneath my tank-top.

"You look great. There's something different about you and I can't get over how amazing you look, Holly."

Trip clears his throat and then throws his arms around my shoulders in a possessive manner. "You better learn how to get over it really fast. She's mine now, and I don't appreciate you staring at her like that."

I smack Trip's washboard abs. "Stop it. Jackson and I are just friends. He's moved on, just like I have."

Trip's eyes burn into mine. "I know you have, baby, but I don't like old friend you used to fuck hanging around you. Don't want them getting any ideas that they can have a taste of what's mine now."

"Trip!" I scold him. "Be nice."

Trip drops his gaze on me and tilts my chin up before planting a kiss on my lips. I close my eyes and decide not to fight him on this as I relax and allow his tongue entrance into my mouth. Everything going through my mind about how to play this in front of Jackson fades away. Jackson clears his throat now and my eyes snap open as the not so subtle sound reminds me this little show is for an audience of one.

Trip grins when he pulls back. "That's just a reminder of what you got last night. No playing nice with the douchebag over there. If he tries to touch you, I'll break his fingers."

Before Trip even fills me in on the next step in the plan, he heads out the front door. I flinch when the screen door bangs shut behind him. I know he's playing the role of jealous boyfriend, but damn if that kiss didn't feel real.

I bite my lip and turn towards Jackson who is studying me, an odd look in his eye. "So that's who you're with now, huh? He doesn't seem like your type, Holl."

I narrow my eyes. "What do you know about my type?"

Jackson takes a step towards me. "I know some overpowering

asshole like that isn't for you. You're better suited with a guy like me."

"What makes you think you're so much better than Trip? He's never cheated on me, which is a lot more than I can say for you."

"I'm beginning to see what I huge mistake that was. I don't like seeing you with someone else."

I fold my arms over my chest. "Well, that's just too damn bad. You should've thought about that before you decided it was a good idea to sleep with other women behind my back."

Jackson nods. "You're right. I was an idiot, but your new boyfriend is never going to give me the chance to make it up to you and earn your love back."

I tilt my head confused. "You're only saying those things to me because you're jealous and don't like that I've found someone else. Besides, Trip doesn't own me. I can talk to whoever I want, whenever I want."

"He's not an idiot, Holl. He can feel the connection between us. He isn't going to let you be alone with me long. But, I'll tell you one thing Trip's got his signals crossed on."

"What's that?"

He steps even closer and reaches up and touches my cheek. "What we had was never just fucking."

My legs grow weak and I fall forward into his waiting arms. It's nice to have confirmation that I actually still mean something to Jackson, even though he became an asshole and pretended like what we had was nothing.

"Jackson—" Before I have a chance to say anything else, he leans in to kiss me. I push my hand into his chest. This feels too fast—plus, how's it going to look if I'm supposedly dating Trip. I can't let Jackson have me again so easy. After what he did to me, he needs to suffer like I did. "Don't."

"You can't be serious about that joker, Holl? Come on. We belong together. You know that. One kiss, for old times' sake."

He tries again, only this time I push him back a little harder. "I mean it, Jackson. I'm with Trip."

He grabs my hips, and tries to pull me into him. I need to get out of here before I let him gain the upper hand—like he always does—and completely ruin everything. If I ever get back together with him, I need to be in charge this time around.

I push him away again. "No, Jackson. It's not going to be that easy. You hurt me and I don't trust you anymore."

Jackson drops his arms to his side. "I deserve that. I'm going to get you back, Holl. I'll be damned if I let another man take what's mine."

I step away from him and lock my gaze with his. "Who is to say he hasn't taken it already."

I don't give Jackson a chance to say another word. I can't risk standing here and allowing him to call bullshit after the plan to make him suffer is already in motion. I turn and walk away.

Jackson calls my name, but I don't bother looking back.

I take a deep breath once I'm on the porch, and am thankful for the space. I need to clear my head and wrap my mind around what the hell just happened in there. Shit went from zero to sixty too fucking fast. My hand rubs my forehead. I need to find Trip and find out what I need to do next. Hopefully I didn't screw things up by pushing him away so harshly.

As soon as my feet hit the gravel in the parking lot, I spot Dad coming out of the garage where we keep extra bikes. He looks worse today. His skin has a sort of grayish tone to it and he moves like he's about ninety instead of forty-seven.

He needs to see a doctor soon.

His feet shuffle over the gravel and smiles the moment he spots me. "Hey, honey. Trip is in garage gearing up to test our track for the first time. Do you mind going out with him? He'll need your expertise. I already hooked him up with some gear."

I nod. "Sure thing. He's who I'm looking for anyhow." We pass each other as we head in opposite directions and I turn towards Dad as he goes by. "Jackson Cruze is in the office."

Dad tilts his head. "You don't say. What's he want?"

I shrug. "He asked me last night if he could come by and ride."

Dad's eyes narrow with suspicion. "You sure he's just here for that and not you."

"Dad," I say, dragging out his name. "Jackson and I are over." Panic hits me as I realize my dad is about to walk in there with my ex who now believes I have a new tattooed, sexy boyfriend. "But, he does think I'm sort of dating Trip."

Dad scratched his head. "Why would he think that?"

"Because Trip and I made Jackson believe we're a couple."

His lips twist. "Why would Trip agree to that?"

"We ran into Jackson at the restaurant last night. After I filled Trip in, he came up with a brilliant plan to make Jackson jealous by pretending to date each other."

He rubs his face. "Honey, I know you've been in love with Jackson for a long time, and he hurt you real bad, but this seems like an awfully dangerous way to go about getting his attention. Sometimes things that start out as a game can get very serious and very out of hand quickly when it comes to playing with people's hearts."

I take a step towards him and throw my arms around his thin shoulders. "We've got it all under control, Dad. Don't worry. I promise no one will get hurt."

He sighs into my hair. "I can't help but worry. You're my baby. I don't like to see you upset."

I hug him tighter. It's nice to know at least one person in this world loves me.

Chapter Seven

"I Said It"

Trip

I yank the black and white jersey over my head and then readjust my vented pants that Bill just gave me to ride in while I'm here. If I go into this business I need to see if Lanie and Aubrey's new advertising company can get the Black Falcon logo on some track wear. That would be badass.

"You look good," Holly says as she walks in the garage. "You look like the real deal."

I glance down at my new gear. "It's pretty sweet. I never knew these pants were part rubber, though."

She leans against the bike I'm standing next to. "Haven't you ridden before?"

"Of course I have, but only for fun, never on a track like this," I admit to her.

She tilts her head. "I was under the impression you were a bike riding expert. That's why your friend, Mr. Snare, hired you."

I laugh. It's kind of cute that she's so clueless. "I'm an expert at many things, but riding a bike isn't one of them. You won't see me doing any crazy jumps today, not that I'd be afraid to learn."

She smiles. "Awesome, now I have something to give you in return for helping me out with Jackson. I'll teach you some basic tricks."

"You can do that shit?" When she nods, I swear she just got a little fucking hotter. "Awesome. I'll take that deal. Speaking of deals, I'm glad things are going well with the asshole."

Holly pinches my arm. "Let's not call him names. He wanted to kiss me. This actually seems to be working pretty well. He's totally jealous."

I grab the helmet off the bike handle and glance over at her. "You didn't let him kiss you, did you?" She shakes her head, and for some crazy reason I feel relieved, which is really fucked up. The plan is working. The guy wants her. I should be thrilled. "Good. Don't let him. You need to play hard to get a while longer."

She licks her lips. "So we need to still pretend to date?"

"Oh, yeah, his suffering has just begun."

She laughs. "I think I'm beginning to enjoy your sadistic way of thinking. Payback is exactly what Jackson needs. This is the best I've felt in a couple weeks."

I tilt my head as I study her. "Are you sure about that? It seemed like you were feeling pretty good at the bar when you were with me."

She throws her hands on her hips. "Are you ever going to let that go? I told you I was drunk. I'm not normally so forward."

I chuckle. "Oh, believe me, sweetness, I learned that yesterday."

Holly wears a smug grin. "Why because I didn't fall for all the lines you threw me about getting into my pants. Being so direct won't always get what you want, you know."

I shove the helmet back onto the handlebar. "Oh, I don't know.

It's worked pretty well for me so far in a lot of aspects of my life." I nod towards the bike that's parked next to mine. "Come show me around this place."

She smiles. "All right. Let me go grab my gear from the house. I'll meet you in the parking lot."

I nod. "I'll push the bike out and wait for you."

Holly turns and walks out of the garage and I can't help but to watch her ass as she leaves. It's pretty fucking great. Too great in my opinion for Jackson—guys like us don't deserve nice girls.

I flick the kickstand down into the gravel and lean against it while I wait on Holly. The screen door on the office slams shut and Jackson comes sauntering out. The suit he's wearing is identical to mine—only I wear it better.

Jackson smirks as he eyes the bike behind me. "You're a rider? How come I've never seen you around here before?"

I pull a pair of sunglasses out of my pocket and slip them on my face. "I'm new in town."

"Is that right?" I don't care for the snide tone in his voice. No one challenges me even a little bit and gets away with it.

I stiffen my back. "Yeah. That's right. What of it?"

Jackson raises his eyebrows. "It's just I know all the riders around here."

"Like I said, I'm new, and to be honest I don't care for the fucking third degree you're trying to give me. If you know what's good for you, you'll back off. Now."

He narrows his eyes at me. "Maybe you don't get how things work around here, so I'm going to fill you in. I run this place. Nothing goes on around here without my okay."

I laugh. "That's funny, because I sure as hell swooped in and stole your girl from under your nose."

He shakes his head. "You and I both know I can get Holly back anytime I want her. When I get tired of fucking around and I'm ready to settle down, she'll take me back. Don't doubt my hold on her. I own her."

My fingers curl into fists at my side. I know the plan is to make him want her back, but after talking to this motherfucker, I know she deserves better. The urge to protect her rages inside me. "That's what you fucking think. I'd like to see you try and take her from me."

Jackson smirks. "Care to place a bet on that?"

Is this asshole for real? He has no idea who in the hell he's challenging. "I don't need to gamble on something that I know is a sure thing."

He steps closer, invading my personal space. "I was with her two years. I could fuck her right in front of you if I wanted."

"Watch your fucking mouth. I swear if you say one more thing about her—"

"You'll what?" he dares me. "Hit me? Do you know who I am, pretty-boy? My lawyers will eat you for breakfast."

His threat doesn't even faze me and it's obvious he has no clue who I am, and that I don't give a fuck about the law. It's never stopped me from ripping into someone's ass before, and it's not going to start now. "Talk about her like that again, and see what happens."

Jackson's tongue touches the corner of his mouth as he wears a smug smile. "You don't know what you've fucking started. I'm going to take her away from you now just because I can. Your days are numbered, prick."

The muscle in my jaw flexes. "Keep telling yourself that, while I'm in her room at night tasting that sweet pussy."

Without warning Jackson sucker punches me square in the nose, knocking the sunglasses off my face. I grab my nose and my eyes water as I stand there stunned. "Motherfucker!"

He bends his knees, and waves his hands at me. "Come on! I'm not through with you."

I wipe the blood away from my nose and smirk. "You hit like a fucking girl. Is that the best you fucking got? You're a dead man!"

I lunge at Jackson but I'm halted in my tracks the moment Holly steps between us and shoves a petite hand into each of our chests. "Stop it! What's wrong with you two?"

Jackson shakes his head and takes a few steps back while staring me down. "You're lucky she saved your ass."

My nostrils flare as I stare him down. The urge to pull Holly out of the way to chase Jackson down to finish what he started rages through every inch of me. I want to rip his fucking head off and spit down his throat, but the second my eyes meet Holly's sad expression I still.

"Let it go, Trip. He's just being a jealous asshole," Holly says as she places both hands on the sides of my face so she can inspect the damage. "Are you okay?"

I glance up at Jackson who seems to be even angrier that Holly has chosen my side. This is the perfect time to drive home the fact that she no longer belongs to him. Playing on her sympathy in front of him will piss him off, which is exactly what I want to do.

I sigh and poke my lip out a little. "I'm okay, but my nose hurts."

She tilts her head and strokes my cheek with thumb. "Let's go get you some ice."

Jackson growls in the background while Holly grabs my hand and pulls me in the direction of the house. A smug smile fills my face as the knowledge that this isn't going to be as easy as he thought fills Jackson's pea-sized brain.

When I decide I want something, no one takes it from me. At this moment I've decided that Holly needs to be mine for the simple fact that I don't want Jackson to have her. That motherfucker doesn't deserve to have her, and I know it fucks with my plan to not get mixed up with her, but damn it, I can't stand the thought of Jackson with her.

I have to do whatever I can to prove to her that she can move on and love someone else—even if that someone else is me.

I know it's selfish reasoning, like a spoiled child not wanting to share toys, but I never claimed to be a saint. And I can't deny that I want her. She's on my mind way too much and it's driving me crazy. Maybe if I get her to like me enough to sleep with me that feeling will go away.

Not since Jessica, has one woman been on my mind for so long and it's got me worried. I thought I was in love with her, but she fucked me over and nearly ruined my entire life with her bullshit. I can't bring myself to trust women again—they can cause insurmountable damage.

The challenge of winning Holly over to spite Jackson is something I have to do. If only for my own selfish pride, I can't let that douchebag win. Making Holly really like me is going to take more than my normal game. I'm going to have to let down my walls and let her in a little to see that I can actually be a nice guy when I want to be.

I close the front door behind us and lead Trip into the living room. The flat pillows on the couch need a good fluffing to be comfortable, so I pick one up and squeeze and rotate it before tossing it back down. "Lie down here while I get that ice for you."

Trip pinches the bridge of his nose and obediently follows my command as I rush off to the kitchen. We don't have an ice pack, so I grab a bag of peas from the freezer. I turn back and head back to Trip. The length of his long legs occupies nearly all the room on the couch and his feet hang off the end. His large hands rest on top of his chest as he lies there with his eyes closed. He looks so peaceful, like he's sleeping, I'm almost afraid to disturb him.

I sit on the edge of the cough at his side and whisper, "Hey. I brought you something for your nose."

He opens his eyes as I lay the small bag across his nose and gives me a small smile. "Thank you."

For some reason the need to comfort him more washes over me. I smooth back the hair on his forehead. "You're welcome. Why did he hit you?"

Trip shrugs. "He told me to stay away from you and I politely refused."

I tilt my head. "Why do I doubt that you do anything nicely?"

"Because I haven't been very nice to you since I got here …" His eyes search my face. "But I want to change that."

I gaze into his green eyes as my heart does a double thump in my chest. "What do you mean?"

He pulls the peas away from his face and props himself up on an elbow, bringing our faces so close his warm breath blows across my lips. "It means I want us to be real friends—not pretend ones, or someone you feel like you have to be nice to out of obligation. I want you to genuinely like me the way I like you."

I lick my lips. "You like me?"

"You know I do. Would I really agree to pretend to date you if I didn't? You're fun to be around and I want to get to know you better."

"That sounds like a good plan. After we punish Jackson enough, and I decide to take him back, we can go on as real friends."

There's tightness in his expression when I mention Jackson. "Are you sure you even want that guy back, Holly? He doesn't seem like he's that into you."

I turn my gaze away from him. "Did he say that?"

Trip puts his index finger under my chin and turns my face towards his. "No, but some of things he said … someone who really cares about you wouldn't say those kinds of things."

I swallow hard. "What did he say?"

"He told me he could take you away from me anytime he wanted because he owned you."

"Is that why you two were fighting?" I question in almost a whisper.

Trip nods. "I don't know what came over me. The things he said, they made me snap and I lost my cool. I said some things I probably shouldn't have. That's why he punched me."

I bite my lip and reach up to touch his face. "Your nose got broken because you were defending my honor?"

He smiles. "I guess so."

His admission of such a sweet gesture moves me. On instinct I lean forward and kiss him softly. "Thank you."

The pull towards him is ridiculous and I know he's a player, but damn it I can't help wanting him. The slippery warmth of his mouth closes over mine and I shut my eyes, enjoying every second.

Desire glazes over his hooded eyes as I pull away. He reaches up and moves a strand of hair away from my face. "You're welcome."

Without warning we throw ourselves together for another kiss. My arms wrap around Trip's neck and he tugs my hips closer. Our tongues whirl together and Trip sits up, cradling me in his arms, pulling me against his chest. One of his hands snake up my back and finds its way into my hair, while I reposition my legs until I'm straddling him.

He groans against my neck as I move my hips, rubbing my crotch over the erection in his jeans. The seam of my shorts presses against my clit and I close my eyes imagining what it would be like if we were naked doing this. I've often wondered what it would be like to be with someone other than Jackson, and Trip makes it feel like it'll be even better than I imagined.

My damp panties cling to my skin as I continue to ride Trip. "God, sweetness. You don't know how much I've thought about this over the last couple of days. It's been so hard to deny myself this."

My tongue darts out and I lick his top lip. "Then stop fighting it."

Trip slides his hands down my body and finds the hem of my riding shirt and tank-top. Soft fingers find their way onto the bare skin of my lower back before working their way up to my breasts. His nimble fingers slide inside one of the cups of my bra and he pushes it down, allowing my nipple to spring free. He rolls my tightened bud between his fingers and licks the inside of my mouth.

"I've been thinking about getting these titties in my mouth all damn day. I imagine everything on your tight little body tastes like heaven. Please tell me that you want this …"

I swallow hard. This is so out of character for me, but for some reason I'm drawn to Trip like crazy. I know it's wrong to want this with him, but my body doesn't understand that. All it knows is that this feels amazing and it can't get enough.

I open my mouth to tell Trip to take me, but my front door opens and I freeze at the sound of Jackson's voice. "Holly? Are you in here?"

I shove Trip's hands out from under my shirt at the same time Jackson walks into the house and spots us. "Jackson? What are you doing in here?"

Jackson's eyes narrow. "I came to apologize for being an asshole, but I can see you both are clearly busy."

I jump up from Trip's lap as Jackson turns and walks out the door. "Jackson, wait! It's not—"

Trip grabs my wrist. "Don't insult him by telling him it isn't what it looks like."

I frown. "Can't you see how hurt he is? I have to find him."

"Let him go, he'll get over it. If you chase him down you might as well be ready to beg him to take you back. Do you really want him to have the upper hand in your relationship again?"

It's second nature to chase Jackson down and apologize to him. I've been doing that over and over for the past year. Every time we fought, he would turn things around and everything would always end up being my fault—just like this situation.

As if Trip can read my mind he says, "It's not you who needs to do the chasing. He cheated on *you*, remember? You aren't together now, we weren't doing anything wrong."

I allow him to tug me back down on the couch and tuck me under his arm. "I hate playing games with people."

He sighs and kisses the top of my head. "You're too sweet for your own good."

Maybe Dad was right. We've just begun this little game and it's already becoming dangerous.

Chapter Eight

"Bringing Down the Giant"

Holly

Trip and I sit in at the front counter together going over more financial documents. Over the last week we've spent every day going over some aspect of this track together. Yesterday I finally got Trip onto the track for the second time. He knows how to handle himself pretty well on a bike. I was impressed with his skills, considering he told me he hasn't been on a bike in a few years. It reminded me of the real reason he's here, and helped me to get over the crazy moment we shared together on the couch.

Jackson hasn't come around the track since the fight last week. Maybe that's for the best. It's good to know it's finally over and he doesn't deem me worthy of fighting for. At least I know where I stand with him.

"I think I'm finally able to decipher Bill's chicken scratch. It's only taken me a week to get it." Trip looks up from the binder full of office expenses he's going through and asks, "Where is Bill? He's been outside washing the bikes for a long time. Do you want me to go check on him?"

I stand and stretch my arms. "That's okay. I'll go do it. I need a break anyhow."

He nods and then returns his attention back to taking notes. I glance up at the clock. Those bikes must've been really dirty—Dad's been out there for nearly four hours.

The garage door is wide open and I hear water slapping the concrete around the corner. I pause the moment my eyes focus on the source of the sound. Jackson is there washing the bikes. I glance around, searching for Dad, but he's nowhere to be seen.

Jackson notices me watching him and shuts off the water before tossing the hose to the ground. He dries his hands on seat of his pants as he approaches me. "Hey, Holl. How are you?"

I twist my fingers together. This is an encounter I'm not prepared for. "I'm good. What are you doing here?"

He shoves his hands deep in his pockets. "I came by to see you, hoping we could talk, but I ran into your dad. He didn't look well, so I told him to go rest and I'd finish up here."

"Thank you. That was sweet of you. He's been like that for a while, but he refuses to go to the doctor," I admit.

"If it's money … I can help with the bills if he needs to be checked out. I don't mind."

I shake my head. "I can't take anything from you, Jackson."

He rubs his hand over his shaved head. "Max told me why that Trip guy is here."

I fold my arms. "That wasn't Max's business to tell."

"Don't be mad at him. He was only trying to help. Max knows I have connections in this business. Why haven't you come to me about this place's money problems?"

I shrug. "By the time I found out how bad things truly were the bank was starting the foreclosure process. There's nothing you could've done at that point. That's why I didn't go back to school this fall. Dad needs my help until this investor comes through."

He frowns. "I wish I would've known that your father was struggling so much. He never said a word about it."

"He's too proud. It was hard for him to tell me. All year at school I didn't have a clue either. Nothing was mentioned until I came home this summer. I had to corner him about why he was a pile of bones and always so stressed. It broke my heart when he told me."

"What happened to all the money from last summer's events? Did he tell you where it went?"

My body tenses and I nod. "He gave it all to *her*."

Jackson's mouth pulls into a tight line. "You mean Grace?"

Visions of the last time I saw of the egg donor pop into my head. She came here with some skinny, grease-ball looking guy in a beat-up pick-up truck, geeking out of her mind. Her blonde hair was clumped together in sections, like it hadn't seen water or soap in weeks, and there were red splotches all over her skin. It was so clear she chose her drug habit over everything thing else in her life—including food. She was so skinny a stiff breeze would knock her over. Nothing else matters to her—not even me—except finding a way to get her next fix. "Yeah. Dad's been an easy mark since I've been away. He's determined to believe my mother is still in there somewhere."

"Jesus," he mutters.

Jackson and Max are my only two friends that know all about my mother, and how my father has spent the better part of half my life trying to save her from herself. I know Trip is searching everywhere in those binders in the office for the answer for why this track is failing, but he's not going to find it in there. There's no place in those files for, "Give all money to drug-addict wife and ruin everyone else's lives".

Tears fill my vision and I drop my head and bat them away. Thinking of Grace does this to me every time. I wish there was a way to wipe someone out of your memory and life for good.

Jackson wraps his arms around me and I cling to him. "Please let me help you? Come to dinner with me tonight. I have a plan to save the track I want to talk to you about."

I sniff. "Okay. Just as friends."

"Of course," he replies.

I rub my eyes. "I don't know why I'm crying."

He doesn't say a word, only tugs me tighter and allows the emotion to flow out of me.

Trip

Holly's been gone a long time. I wonder if Bill is okay? I've gotten to know the routine around here pretty well over the last week, and for Bill to take this long to do anything is out of character. He's a hard worker, but gets gassed easily. I can't count the number of times Holly has begged her father to go to the doctor, and I've even found myself taking her side on the topic.

Spending all my time with Bill and Holly reminds me of how nice having a regular life with a family can be, but it also brings on the concern you feel for others well-being. On the road it's easy just to care about myself and the other guys in the band. It feels so surreal that it's easy to pretend everyone else's problems don't exist—only finding concern when it affects me directly.

I make my way outside towards the garage. My mouth drops open when I round the corner and find Holly wrapped in Jackson's arms. Her head rests against his chest as he strokes the back of her blonde head. A lump builds in my throat knowing the connection I felt with her this past week has meant nothing to her, and she's going right back to that jackass.

Jackson's eyes whip in my direction and he smirks over Holly's head so she can't see his expression while he flips me off. His way of saying he won makes my blood boil. My instinct drives me to rip Holly away from her and find a way to make her stay away from him and ask her to give me a chance. Can't she see how much I want her?

I sigh and back away. Jackson's smile grows wider. As much as I want her, I won't try to force her to like me back the same way. I can't even explain why I want her so much—I just know that I do. I haven't had this much fun with a woman in a long time.

I turn and head to the house, not wanting to see her with him anymore.

Inside their house I hear the soft noise of the television playing in the living room. Bill's sitting in the recliner, covered in a blanket, the remote in his hand. His color is grayer than normal, and his blue eyes appear to be sunken in a little.

I sit on the couch across from him. "You don't look good, Bill. I think it's time you give into Holly and get yourself to the doctor."

"Can't," is all he says.

In good conscience I can't sit her and allow a man to compromise his health because he doesn't have the money to pay his doctor to check him out. Something has to give. "Bill, if I tell you something, do you promise not to get angry and to keep the secret between us?"

He readjusts in his chair. "Depends on how bad it is."

I laugh. "It's nothing bad—more like something about myself I want to keep private."

"If that's the case, I have no problem with that. We all have things we don't want other people to know."

I rub my face and let out a deep breath. It's now or never. "I'm the investor."

Bill raises his eyebrows. "You? Why wouldn't you lead us to believe it was your friend?"

"I didn't want who I am to complicate things? I wanted to come here and get a look first hand at the business and to get to know you," I admit.

He tilts his head. "Who exactly are you, Trip?"

"I'm the drummer for Black Falcon."

"Wow ..." Bill trails off. "I wasn't expecting that. I can't say I've heard your music, but those entertainment shows sure mention your band a lot." He glances around his house. "I bet you're used to staying in places a lot better than this."

I chuckles. "I suppose so, but hotels don't have the charm this place does."

"Ah, charm. What you mean to say is they don't have Holly." He lowers his gaze at me.

I lick my lips. "I'll admit, I like your daughter, but I don't think she feels the same way about me."

"She likes you, trust me. I know enough about my daughter to know that."

I sigh. "Even if she does, I think she likes Jackson more."

Bill shakes his head. "Those two have history, and Holly is still young. She doesn't know how to let go of a love that is no longer there. We have that in common. Give it time. Jackson will disappoint her again. He always does."

"I don't know, Bill. They looked pretty cozy a few minutes ago."

Bill crosses his legs at the ankles. "That's Jackson for you. The boy never did share well with others. Take this track for instance—thinks he owns it, like he can do whatever he wants here. Chases off riders he doesn't want around. The boy has cost me a lot of business, running off any guy that stared at Holly a little to long, but I didn't say much because I knew Holly loved him. That all changed a few weeks ago when he came here to call it quits with my daughter. I told that little asshole that as long as there was still a breath left in my body, I owned this place."

"I've noticed you've been sick the entire time I've been here. Why don't you want to go to the doctor, Bill? If it's money, don't worry about that. I'll see to it that this place gets insurance, and I pay for any medical bills you may get until then."

Bill shakes his head. "I can't let you do that, Trip. What I have isn't curable. It would be a waste of your money."

My brow furrows. "You mean you already know there's something wrong with you?"

He nods while wearing a solemn expression. "I have HIV."

A gasp leaves my body. I've never actually known someone with that virus, and I never would've expected an upstanding family man like Bill Pearson to have it. My eyes trace down Bill's frail body, and things start to click. "Why haven't you told Holly?"

Tears well up in his eyes, and he bats one away as it slips down his face. "Because there's nothing she can do to fix it. My girl is a fixer, and it'll destroy her because she can't fix this. I would rather things take their natural course and she find out after I'm gone. It'll be easier that way."

He's right about Holly, but that doesn't change the fact that she should know. "Easier for who? You or her?"

He shrugs. "For both of us. I don't want to hurt my baby. The thought that I'll probably leave her sooner rather than later crushes me."

"How long have you had it?" I ask.

"My wife, Grace, contracted the virus about fifteen years ago and gave it to me. I think now since I stopped getting my medications last year, things are getting worse."

"Is that Holly's mom? Is she still alive?" I've wondered about where her mother is, but I never asked because I figured it wasn't my business.

"Yes, if you want to call what she does living. She's a heroine addict. After Grace cheated on me and discovered she'd given me HIV, she couldn't handle the guilt. She ran off—cut pretty much all contact with Holly and me, except when she's out of money. That's when she comes around. When she's desperate to find a way to get her next fix, she comes home, and I always give in."

I shake my head. That's so fucking sad. I know Noel Falcon's drug use once destroyed Black Falcon. Thank God Riff was able to get through to Noel before he got in too deep and ruined his life. "Jesus, I'm sorry. Drugs can royally screw a person's life up. That's a shame."

"That's what Holly used to say, but as she got older the emotion she felt towards her mother went from sympathy to anger. The last few years, every time Grace has come around, Holly chases her away and won't allow her to speak to me. I was grateful to her, I could never tell Grace, "No", but Holly is a lot stronger than me. She stands up for what's right. She's special."

The weight of this secret presses down on my heart. How is this fair that I know this about her father and she doesn't? Bill's right. Holly *is* special. I knew it when I first laid eyes on her in the club. She stood out to me against all the other women vying for my attention—and she wasn't even trying. That easy smile she wore when she hugged Max—

the way she cut loose on the floor—I knew I had to have her and I didn't even care if she was with another guy. That goes against everything I stand for. I hate cheaters. I was screwed over, so I know how bad it sucks. Cheating nearly ruined my life, but none of that even entered my brain because something about Holly drew me in and I was powerless to fight against it.

The inner turmoil must be easy to see on my face. Bill leans forward in his chair and catches my gaze. "Trip, neither of us wants Holly to find out what we're keeping from her, so the only way I'll promise to keep your secret is if you keep mine."

I stare at this selfless man, who loves his daughter so much he's willing to shield that he's dying to save her some heartache. My heart cracks at the thought of how painful this must be for him. I don't want to see Holly or Bill hurting. There has to be something I can do.

"Bill, I'm ready to agree to be your partner in this business, I'll shake on it right now if you agree to allow me to pay for your doctor visits and medications. I want to keep you here for Holly as long as I can." I know I can't make this all go away, but considering the cards that have been dealt before me, it's the best offer I can come up with. "Please let me do this for you."

He doesn't answer right away, just stares at the television absently for a few moments, but then he nods. "Okay. I'd be a fool to turn a deal like that down."

I give him a small smile and extend my hand to him. "Do we have a deal?"

Bill's hand meets mine. "We do, partner."

And just like that I've agreed to take on half of the tracks problems in the hopes that someday we'll be able to turn this place around and actually see a profit.

Tyke is going to ream me out for making such a hasty decision.

He won't understand that this just felt like the right thing to do. I've got to go with my gut on this one. I believe I can make a real difference here, so this is where I need to be.

Chapter Nine

"She Will Be Loved"

Holly

I study the way the blue dress hugs my curves in the mirror. This isn't exactly a "we're purely platonic" outfit but it's perfect for torturing Jackson some more. I almost feel bad about playing this game with him now, but when I allow myself to think about him sleeping with other women behind my back it relieves the guilt, and keeps pushing me to act indifferent towards him.

"I love the color of that dress," Max says as he glances up from a magazine while lying on my bed. "Blue has always been your color. It matches your eyes. But I wish you weren't wearing it to impress the asshole."

I smooth the dress down. "Do you think it's wrong to make someone jealous on purpose?"

"If you're talking about making Jackson jealous, then you already know my answer. You know how I feel about him."

I put my hands on my hips. "What if I am? How would that affect your answer?"

Max closes the magazine and tosses it next to him. "That asshole doesn't deserve any more of your energy. He cheated on you, Holly. Then said he didn't love you. Don't let him mess with your head just because you've got something going with the new meat in town. Jackson's fucked with your head long enough. He always strings you along. It's time to move on, and maybe Trip's the guy to do that with."

"I thought you said he's not the right kind of guy for me? What's with the sudden change of heart?"

Max throws his legs over the edge of the bed. "I've seen you two together. The way both of you look at the other … I don't know … it's weird, like you have some sort of connection. I think I was wrong about him. Besides, I don't care much for Jackson threatening to beat my ass if I didn't tell him everything I knew about Trip. That jerk is the biggest fucking bully. I can't understand what you ever saw in him."

"I'm sorry he did that to you. He can be an asshole sometimes, I know." I sit next to Max, my heart feeling heavy that I've been keeping things from him about Trip. "If I tell you something, promise not to yell at me?"

He tilts his head. "When have I ever yelled at you?"

I laugh. "Okay, maybe you don't yell, but you certainly like to try and change my mind when you think I'm doing something bad."

"I only do that because I love you, Holl. And, yes, I firmly believe if you would take my advice more often where men are concerned you'd be happier."

I sigh. "I know, which is why I need your advice now."

Max twists his lips. "I'm all ears."

I clutch my hands together in my lap. "Trip and I aren't actually dating."

His brow furrows. "What do you mean? You told me last week Jackson and Trip got into it because Jackson is jealous you're dating

Trip. I don't understand."

I take a deep breath. "I know that's what I said, but the truth is, we've sort of been *pretending* to be an item."

Max leans his head back and groans. "Oh no. Tell me you didn't rope Trip into making Jackson jealous."

I grimace. "It was his idea."

"And you thought it was a good one? When did you make this little deal?"

"The day after we met him at the bar."

"So *after* you kissed him?"

I nod. "Yes." Max laughs and I smack his leg. "Why is that so funny?"

"You honestly think you two can pretend to like each other without real emotions getting involved?" I open my mouth to answer, but he cuts me off. "I saw you two at the bar, remember. That's attraction, babe, and you can only fight that for so long. This is going to blow up in your face."

"So you think what Trip and I are doing is a mistake?"

He shakes his head. "No. I think trying to win *Jackson* back is a mistake. Trip seems to be really into you. I'd rather you see where that leads."

"Where is this coming from? Aren't you the one who warned me off of him a couple weeks ago?"

"I was, but that was before I saw the two of you together."

"Even if I think I might have feelings for Trip, he's leaving, so they won't matter. I don't want to develop feelings for a guy that's not even going to stick around."

"You don't know that. He might be willing to leave everything behind to move out here if things work out."

"That's crazy talk, Max. I only know the very basics about him. I know he's from Kentucky, has a twin brother, and his parents are still married. Other than that, I don't know a thing about him. I don't even know if he has a real job."

"Well, why don't you ask him?"

"You think it's that simple?"

"Yes. Yes, I do. Trip should be the one you're going out on a date with tonight, not Jackson. You like him. Admit it and get to know him."

"I told you, this isn't a date with Jackson. He has a way to help the track, so this is a business dinner."

Max rubs his chin. "Then why didn't he tell you to bring your dad along?"

I have no answer to that, really. That's a great question. "I don't know. Maybe he feels more comfortable just talking to me about it first?"

He raises his eyebrow. "He's known your dad just as long as he's been coming to this track. Face it. Jackson is a spoiled toddler who doesn't like to share his toys. If he really loved you, Holly, it wouldn't take another man showing an interest in you to make him remember that. People want what they can't have. It'd be smart of you to remember that."

What he says makes perfect sense, yet the curiosity to see how Jackson thinks we can save the track wins out. "You're probably right, but I still need to go."

Max reaches over and holds my hand in his lap. "Just be careful, would you? I don't want to get my ass kicked when I try and go beat those two jerks up over hurting you. Believe it or not, I'm delicate."

I laugh and pat his hand. "You're such a good friend."

He grins. "That's what a best friend is for."

After I double check myself in the mirror, Max and I head

downstairs. The heavenly aroma of sizzling steak fills the lower level of the house. Dad is fast asleep, curled up under a blanket in his recliner while Trip is busy in the kitchen, cooking. I study my father, he looks so much older than he did even five years ago. It makes me sad he doesn't take better care of himself. He's all I have left and I wish he would at least make an effort to get well for me.

"You two are just in time. The food is nearly done. Hope you guys like your steaks medium, if not I can leave them on a little longer," Trip says as he glances over his shoulder. "Can you grab me a plate for these, Holly?"

My heels click against the wood floor as I walk to the cabinet. I hand him the plate. "This is so sweet of you."

Trip shrugs. "We're celebrating."

I raise an eyebrow because my curiosity is killing me. "Oh? What might that be?"

He slaps the steaks on the plate and smiles. "Mountain Time Speed Track has an investor."

"Really?!" I squeal and throw my around his neck. "That's amazing news!"

He laughs and sets the food down before turning and wrapping his arms around my waist. The expression on his face turns serious the moment he takes in my outfit. "You look amazing. Are you going out somewhere?"

I nod. "Jackson has an idea to help save the track, so I'm meeting him for dinner to talk about it."

His lips pull into a tight line. "Call and cancel. You don't need his help anymore."

"Trip … I can't do that. Your investor friend signing on is great, but we need ways to drum up business. I have to hear what Jackson has to say. We need all the help we can get around here." Trip opens his mouth, but quickly closes it when a horn honks twice outside. "That's him. We'll talk more tonight."

I lean up and kiss his cheek before running out the door and hoping in Jackson's car.

The familiar scent of leather and woodsy cologne assaults my nose as soon as I close the door, locking myself in with Jackson. I used to love this smell. Sitting in here now reminds me of a time when being with Jackson was very comforting, instead of the tension I feel being next to him now. I can't help but wonder how many other women he has had in this very seat behind my back, and a mixture of sadness and anger wash over my heart.

"Wow! That's some dress, Holl. It's tight in all the right places," Jackson says, his eyes appraising my outfit.

Typically that kind of compliment would have had me giggling like an idiot, but now it rubs me the wrong way, like all he's interested in is my body. I remember those kinds of remarks being a lot sweeter. That is before I found out he was using them on every other girl around here.

I tug the hem of the dress down to cover my thighs a little better. "Thanks, I think."

Jackson backs out of the parking lot and then turns in the direction of downtown Tucson before reaching over and taking my hand in his. "I'm so glad you decided to come out with me tonight. Things are going to be good this time, Holly. I promise."

I withdraw my hand from his. "I only agreed to come out with you for the track, Jackson. This is just business."

He readjusts in his seat, staring straight ahead. "Business it is, then."

Neither of us says another word during the ride. Tension rolls around us, but I won't be the one to break it. He asked me to come out with him. He knows we aren't together, and it's unfair of him to think I would just give in and be an easy lay.

Once we're seated at the small table in the restaurant, Jackson says, "This is awkward. Maybe this was a mistake. We can leave."

Panic washes through me as I realize he might not help unless I give in a little. "Let's start over. I'd like us to be friends."

Jackson toys with the fork in front of him. "Friends, huh? You know, that night in your room, I was hoping we could part as friends, so I could move on without a guilty conscience, but when I hear you say it—it stings."

I sigh. "Jackson ... *you* chose to end things."

"I know, and I'm here to say I made a mistake. I want you to take me back, Holly. You know we're good together. Things could go back to how they were and I can help you set up a motocross competition to draw a crowd to the track."

I shake my head. "I don't want things to go back to how they were."

His brow pulls in. "Don't you want to get back together?"

This is the moment I've been wanting—for Jackson to come crawling back, admitting he was wrong—so why don't I feel excited? I take a deep breath and Trip's face pops into my head, which puzzles me. Why would I be thinking of him at a time like this?

As if Jackson is poking around in my brain, he asks, "Is it because of Trip?"

My eyes widen at his forwardness. "No. Well, I mean, a little, yes, but the main reason I don't want to take you back has to do with you."

"Me?" he asks with a surprised face. "I admitted I made a mistake by fooling around on you, and I'm sorry. Can't we just move past that?"

I shake my head. "You don't get it, do you? It's not just the fact that you cheated—that's just *one* of the reasons. You lied to me. I bet it went on a lot longer than you lead me to believe. You probably just got tired of hiding it all the time." He opens his mouth to argue, but I don't give him the opportunity, and the reasons I don't want him back flow freely from my mouth. "You never supported the idea of me going away to college, even though I had my heart set on it. And I don't like how you treat Max."

His eyes narrow. "What do you mean?"

"I don't like you harassing my friend. Max told me you threatened him if he didn't tell you why Trip was here."

"I only did that because I was worried about the guy's intentions. I don't like to see you get hurt."

I laugh sarcastically. "That's rich. You can hurt me but no one else can."

Jackson's jaw muscle flexes under his skin. "You know what, Holly, I'm done."

"You're done? What does that even mean?"

"It means that I lost my mind believing that I wanted you back. Tell Trip he won and he can have your bitchy ass." He rises from the table.

"Where are you going?"

"I'm leaving. Find your own way home." Jackson throws a twenty on the table. "That should cover your meal."

My mouth drops open as I watch him turn and leave the restaurant. I can't believe that asshole just left me stranded here. Max was right. I'm beginning to question my own judgment on what I ever saw in that guy.

The petite, blonde waitress approaches the table. "Would you like to order your drinks now, or are we waiting on someone else?"

I dig in my purse and hand her my fake ID. "It's just me, and I would like to start with something from the bar."

Trip

The way Holly tore out of here made my heart sink. I know her goal is getting Jackson back, and I'm a dumbass for beginning to care about a girl who loves someone else, but I wish she would reconsider that asshole. The idea that he could be kissing those sweet lips of hers right now makes my blood boil. I've tasted those lips, and all I've done over the past week is thought about doing it again.

I stab the steak in front of me with my fork and vigorously begin cutting it, while picturing Jackson's smug face.

"Whoa. What did that thing ever do to you?" Max asks.

I shrug. "Nothing. I was just thinking."

"About Holly and Jackson," Max prods before taking a bite.

My eyes flick to his, but I don't answer. I don't need him knowing my business.

Max takes a drink of water and then sets his glass down. "I never did like the guy."

"Why?" I ask and then take another bite before glancing over at Bill, who is still asleep in the recliner. "I thought you all were friends or something."

"Or something …" Max says. "Jackson Cruze is a narrow-minded homophobe who talks with his fists."

"You two have gotten into it before?"

Max nods. "Oh, yeah, many times."

I raise an eyebrow. "And Holly stayed with him. I thought girl-code was if the boyfriend and the best friend didn't get along, the guy didn't last long."

Max shrugs. "I never told her."

"Why not?"

"I might be gay, Trip, but I still have pride like any other man. I don't want everyone to know I get my ass beat every time I turn around, especially not my female best friend who treats me more like a man than most people around here do."

"I thought no one knows your ... sexual orientation."

"I've never officially come out if that's what you mean, but people have speculated for a long time now."

I take a deep breath. "You still should've told Holly what a dick Jackson has been to you."

He shakes his head. "I wanted her to open her eyes to what an asshole he is on her own. Holly is hard-headed, and if I'd tried to tell her things about Jackson that she wasn't ready to hear, she wouldn't have believed them. She's the kind of girl that has to see things with her own eyes. Like that old saying goes, love is blind."

"So I've heard." I swallow down the last bite of my food and lean back in the chair, thinking about all the crazy shit Black Falcon has been through with Noel and Riff and all their women bullshit. Those two guys never listen to my advice in the matters of the heart. It's like they're too caught up in their own drama to see reason.

Max's cell vibrates against the table, and I can clearly see Holly's name across the caller ID. I pick up the phone without asking his permission and answer, swatting his hand away. "How's your date?"

"Trip? Why are you answering Max's phone?" The confusion in her voice rings clear.

"We're here enjoying these delicious steaks you ran out on. Where are you?" She sniffs into the phone and I realize she's crying. I stiffen in my chair. "What's wrong? Did Jackson hurt you?"

My hand tightens around the phone at the exact moment Max pushes away from the table and heads out the door. I watch through the window as he gets into his car and tears out of the driveway. I probably should ask where he's going, but whatever it is, it's his business.

"No. He didn't hurt me, but he left me here at Paulo's. Can you ask Max to come and get me?"

My heart pounds in my chest. The thought of Holly being alone and stranded hits me hard. Bad things can happen to women left alone in a vulnerable state. The next time I see Jackson, he's a dead man. "I'll come and get you. Stay put inside the restaurant," I order.

"Okay," she agrees before she disconnects the phone.

I lay Max's phone on the table and search my own out of my pocket. I look up the restaurant's address in my phone and then plug it into my phone's GPS. Two minutes later I'm on the road, following the digital voice's directions.

I pull up to Paulo's and cut the engine. The little Mexican joint is hoping with a party inside. A DJ in the corner both spins the top pop hit of the week, and bodies pack the small dance floor.

Jackson brought her *here* to discuss track business? He obviously doesn't really give a shit about Mountain Time. What a fucking douchebag.

I weave in and out of the bodies until I spot Holly alone at a corner table for two, sipping on a drink. There's a deep frown on her face while she watches everyone around her. She sticks out sitting there all alone in a room full of people having a good time and I get the sudden urge to lift her sprits.

The second I reach her table the song *Smooth* by Santana plays over the speakers and I think back to the first time I saw her and what a good time she was having that night in the bar. I'll do anything to see that smile again.

I extend my hand and her blue eyes trail up my arm and cheat until they meet mine. "Dance with me."

Holly sets her drink down and places her hand in mine, allowing me to pull her up and lead her to the floor. The sexy guitar chorus screams as I pull her against me without permission. Both of her arms wrap around my neck and my hands slide down her back before resting on her slim hips. We rock in time to the beat, our eyes glued to one another's, neither of us speaking a word while our bodies do all the talking.

Her mouth drops open when I allow my hands to wander down and grab a hold of her ass. I fully expect her to pull away and give me the evil eye, but she doesn't. Instead, she shocks me by licking her lips in anticipation.

Holy mother of God.

Those lips. They're all I've been dreaming about, but didn't want to push her into fooling around with me again unless she wants to.

She presses up on her tiptoes and whispers in my ear, "Does your invitation from the first time we danced about taking me home still stand? I'm tired of thinking about Jackson. Make me forget about him like I know you want to."

Holly licks my earlobe once before sucking on it. My eyes roll back in my head. She has no clue how much that fucking turns me on. I only have so much self-control

I pull back and stare into her eyes. If I had to guess, she's had a few drinks, but not enough to completely impair her judgment—just enough to loosen her up. I want her, but I want her to want me for the right reasons, not because she's lonely and needs somebody.

Sensing my hesitation, she grabs each side of my face, pulling me down to kiss my lips. "If you want me to say please, I will. I know how you like women that beg."

My cock jerks and I groan as I rub her ass. "You don't know how much I want you."

She wiggles her hips, rubbing her pelvis against mine and she grins. "I think I have a pretty good idea."

That little naughty glint in her eyes is enough to allow my brain to say, "Fuck all the logical reasoning for not giving her what she's asking for." I thread my fingers in her hair and plant my lips on hers. She opens her mouth and allows my tongue entrance so I deepen our kiss.

I fucking want her. I know I shouldn't and I've been fighting against this very thing happening since I found out who she was, but ever since the last taste I had of her on the couch, this is all I've been thinking about. I just didn't want to seem like a pushy asshole bringing up the situation, especially since she was doing her best to pretend that nothing ever happened between us.

I pull back and stare into her lust-filled eyes before pulling her arms from around my neck and leading her out of the restaurant. I can't wait any longer.

The moment we reach the Mustang, I spin Holly around and back her against the car. My mouth crashes into hers. She's even sweeter than I remember and it's fucking addicting.

I kiss a trail down her jaw line and nibble on the sensitive skin below her ear. Holly throws her head back and moans as I work my way back to her mouth.

"I want you, Trip. Take me home," she says in a breathy voice.

I pull her forward and reach behind her, opening the car door. "Get in," I order.

The entire fifteen-minute ride, Holly has her seatbelt off and leans across the console, rubbing my thigh while teasing me with kisses. We pull down into the driveway and my headlights shine on the house. Fuck. I can't very well have my way with her upstairs while her ill father lays downstairs and has to listen to that. I'm not that fucking disrespectful.

As if Holly read my mind, she whispers in my ear, "Let's go into the office."

I hop out of the car and run around to the passenger side to let Holly out of the car. She threads her fingers through mine and leads me to the office. I take a deep breath and try to calm myself down as she unlocks the door and pulls me inside. Tonight is all about the two of us. I want to show her that she can trust me and that we are good together.

Chapter Ten

"Gorilla"

Holly

The moment we're inside the office, Trip's hands are everywhere. He's tugging on my clothes and threading his fingers in my hair, pulling me deeper into his kiss. I've never felt so wanted and desired before. It's like he can't get enough of me and I love the way that makes me feel.

He backs me up against the counter and runs his hands down my bare shoulder, then down my torso, before finally settling on my hips. He grips my waist and hoists me onto the counter with ease. The hem of my blue dress stretches and it creeps up my thighs as Trip pushes himself between my legs. His lips attack mine again and I throw my hands in his hair to try and immerse myself in him more.

Trip wraps his arms around me and tugs me closer, but never stops kissing me. The weight of his body rubbing against me causes me to tingle all over. My panties grow wet as the sensation of the ridged material of his jeans presses against the sensitive flesh between my legs.

I'd be lying to myself if I say I haven't wanted this with him since that night in the bar. No man has ever been able to make me aroused this quickly. There's just something about him that's very animalistic and I'm drawn to his take-charge attitude. The way he blatantly wants me is such a turn on. This is a man that goes for exactly what he wants and doesn't make any excuses about it, which makes it even crazier that it's me he wants. Every woman desires that.

"God, you're all I want, Holly. I've dreamed of this moment since I first kissed you," Trip says. "You're the only woman that's ever drove me crazy like this."

Every instinct in my body is telling me he's telling the truth. I can't explain it, only that I feel it. It's then I realize it's him. It's been him for a while now. Jackson has only been my excuse to allow acting on the attraction I've felt for him since that night in the club. I've wanted Trip for so long. All those nights lying awake in my room at night I spent dreaming of him should've told me that. If I really loved Jackson, I wouldn't have been giving Trip a second thought.

I pull back and stare into his green eyes. "Trip …" I say his name almost like a whisper. "I …" I pause. I can't just come out and tell him I think I have feelings for him. What if this has all been just a big game for him. I can't chance it. I don't want my heart crushed.

Trip grabs my face in his hands, rubbing his thumbs against my cheeks. "You *what*, Holly? Tell me. I need to hear you say it."

I hesitate. "What do you want me to say?"

He swallows hard and pulls our faces close enough for me to feel his breath on my lips. "If you feel something for me, tell me now. Please, tell me because I can't stop thinking about you and I don't know what to do about it."

I close my eyes and touch my forehead to his. "This is so complicated."

"It doesn't have to be. Just say the words. Tell me you don't want to be with Jackson, that you really want me. I don't think I can stand by and watch him touch you one more goddamn day. You belong with me."

How can I not tell him I feel the same way after he's laid out his feelings so clearly. I open my eyes to meet his gaze. I grab the hem of his shirt and tug him closer to me. "It's you that I want. Not Jackson."

That's all it takes for Trip to crush his lip to mine. This kiss is different. It's more intense, and I can tell where this one is leading, there's no going back.

Trip's hand roams under my dress and his fingers find the wet spot on my underwear. "You don't know how fucking sexy that is and how badly I want a taste."

My toes try to curl inside my stilettos and my body is too turned on to worry about being shy now. "Then what's stopping you?"

A devilish smile creeps onto his face. "I love a bossy woman." He kisses my lips. "Lift your ass up."

I raise my hips as he ordered and he shoves my dress up around my waist before ripping my panties. I hiss as he pulls the fabric from my body. He's taking what he wants and not apologizing for it. There's nothing sexier than that.

Trip tugs the straps of my dress over my shoulders and then pulls the top of my dress down. The warmth of his hands is amazing as he kneads my breasts on the outside of my bra. The index and middle fingers of his right hand slip inside and push my bra down, revealing my puckered pink nipple. After he does the same thing to the other side he kisses a trail down my throat before heading further south and sucking on my nipple. I allow my head to fall back and I sigh as I run my fingers through his hair.

He drops to his knees and grabs my ass, yanking my pussy closer to his mouth. "The first time I fuck you, it's going to be fast. I won't last once I slip inside you. I've wanted this too damn long. There's no way I can hold back. But the second time I'm going to go slow, so I can savor every inch of that beautiful body of yours."

He doesn't give me any time to debate him on the issue. The heat of his tongue against my throbbing clit is almost more than I can handle. After a few flicks, my legs resting over his shoulders begin to shake. I grab his hair as a tingle erupts and then spreads completely over my body.

"Oh, God," I moan as my body erupts in complete euphoria.

Trip stands and kisses my lips, allowing me to taste myself on him. "Watching you come is even hotter than I imagined. I can't wait to bury myself inside you."

He reaches in his pocket and pulls out a condom before unzipping his pants. I lean up and shove his jeans and boxers down around his ass. His large cock springs free and I wrap my hand around it and begin to playfully stroke him while he opens the wrapper.

He hands me the rubber. "Put it on me."

I take the slippery condom from him and pinch the tip as I roll it down his shaft to the base. Trip's hooded eyes rake over my body as I lean back on my elbows and open my legs for him. I'm so turned on by the look on his face. It's as if he can't take his eyes off me.

Trip leans down and kisses my lips. "You don't know how much I've thought about you just like this. I promised myself I wouldn't fuck you, but damn it, I can't help myself. I'm a selfish bastard and I can't make myself not want you."

I melt into him and wrap my legs around his waist before attacking his lips. "I want you too—ever since that night in the club."

He groans as he penetrates me with the head of his cock. "So fucking tight. If I didn't know better, I would think you're a virgin."

"Don't be gentle," I whisper, wanting to feel him moving inside me.

Trip pushes his entire length in and then pulls it back out so he can do it again. "You feel so fucking good. I don't want this to end."

"It doesn't have to," I say.

"Promise?" He asks, staring into my eyes.

I nod and he picks up the pace, pumping into me faster and harder. After a few minutes sweat slicks his skin, and I run my hands up and down his back as his balls slap against me.

I stare up at his face and watch him bite his lip, like he's trying to make this last as long as he can while he gazes at me. The idea of him enjoying the way I feel causes another orgasm to rip through me.

"Trip!" I cry out his name and his movements become more ridged and intense.

"Ah, fuck. Yeah." He follows my release with his own and collapses on top of me, peppering my face with soft kisses. "You are so fucking amazing."

I giggle beneath him and play with the wild strands of hair poking out from his head. "I have to say that was a first for me."

Trip raises his head and looks me in the eye. "What was?"

I shrug. "An orgasm."

His eyes widen. "You've never had one before?"

"Oh, I have, just never with someone else involved." A blush creeps over my cheeks as I admit that out loud.

"Really?" He lifts an eyebrow and grins. "Get ready, sweetness. There's a whole lot more where that came from. I'm the self-proclaimed Orgasm King."

I laugh. "By yourself doesn't count."

He shifts his hips and slides his still erect shaft back and forth inside me. "You know it's true. I just gave you two in less than fifteen minutes."

"Mmm … maybe you better show me again so I can see if you warrant that title," I tease.

"It'll be your pleasure." He smirks as he goes to work kissing on my neck.

Trip

Holly leans back against my chest and I wrap my arms around her before kissing the top of her head. It's been a long time since I've cuddled like this after sex. Normally I stick to fucking in a neutral space so I can easily escape without all the expected sappy time after the fun. But this time is different. I *want* to be here with Holly. In fact, just like I was afraid of, now that I've gotten a real taste of her sweetness, I'm fucking addicted.

She traces light circles on my forearm with the tips of her fingers. "What are you thinking about?"

I sigh. "About how I'll never be able to leave this place now."

"Oh?" I hear the curiosity in her voice. "Why's that?"

"Because of you," I answer truthfully. "You're a pretty amazing woman."

She turns in my arms and throws her legs over one of mine while we sit on the shop's counter. "I'll never be able to look at this counter again. Every time I see it, I'll think of you … us … and tonight."

"Who says it has to be just tonight?" I ask with optimism. "I'd be willing to stick around a little longer."

She turns her gaze up to mine. "Don't you have bands to manage?

Won't they miss you?"

I shrug. "They're kind of on break right now. Besides, maybe if you and I work out, you'd come on the road with me for a while, after we get this business back on the right track."

She shakes her head. "I don't know, Trip. Being around famous people just isn't my thing. I'm just not into the whole drug and party scene—not to mention what jackasses they are. Look at Jackson for crying out loud. He's just gotten a little taste of fame and he's so full of himself he can barely see straight."

My heart sinks. "Not all famous people are like that, and for the record, I'm almost positive Jackson's always been a douchebag."

"You're right. I don't know how I missed it all these years. I guess now I understand why my dad won't listen to reason about my mom. He still loves her after everything she's done to him—us—and lets her walk all over him. I never understood why he did that, but I guess I've been sort of doing the same thing with Jackson. He's never really treated me very well."

"I'm glad you got away from him, and who knows, maybe your dad will wise up one day too."

"I don't think he will. He's still giving her money, which is a bad thing considering she's a drug addict."

"Bill told me about her," I say, not wanting to pretend that I don't already know Bill and Grace's history.

"What did he say?" she whispers.

My stomach ties in a knot as I think about Bill trusting me with his HIV secret, and making me promise not to tell Holly or he'll expose my identity to her, which would be bad. She just sat here and said she hates people like me. I need more time to prove to her I'm a decent guy. I like having her around, and I want to keep it that way.

She's still waiting on me to answer her, so I say, "Not much, just that the two of you no longer get along and he talked a little about why that was."

"I can hardly look at her. She doesn't even look like my mom anymore. Every time she comes around, I'm reminded of how she chose drugs over us, and despite everything my dad is always willing to help her. I just don't understand. I'm so scared I'll be like her someday. That's why I went away to college and was studying psychology. I guess I was hoping if I understood why addicts do the things they do, I would be able to stop that from happening to me."

I tip her chin with my finger, making her look up at me. "You won't be like her. You're too smart for that."

Holly gives me a sad smile. "I hope you're right."

"I know I am." I kiss her lips.

She bats away a tear from her eye. "I'm sorry I'm crying. I know that's a guy's worst nightmare after sex."

I wipe another tear from her beautiful face. "Holding you in my arms is far from a nightmare, Holly. I'm glad you're opening up to me. It means you trust me."

"I do trust you. I know I gave you a hard time when you first got here, but that's only because I love this track and I didn't think someone who looked like you could care about this place the way I do. You've proved me wrong since you've been here, putting all the work into getting to know everything about the place and us. I never did thank you for convincing your friend to go into business with Dad. That was really amazing, so … thank you."

"You're welcome." I smile.

"I still don't know much about you though. Tell me something about yourself—something personal."

I clear my throat. If I want to be with this girl she might as well know the darkest details about me. "I was married once."

She instantly stiffens in my arms. "Ma—married? When?"

"I was nineteen, and stupid. It didn't end well."

"What happened?" Holly asks as she sits up straighter in my arms.

I pinch a strand of her blonde hair between my fingers and twirl it as I gather my thoughts. "The typical thing that happens to most marriages involving young people—she found someone else, but neglected to tell me about it until I caught them together."

She gasps. "That's terrible! You found them in bed together?"

"No. I used to play in a band, and when we took a quick break, I found Jessica, my wife at the time, practically fucking some dude in the corner of the bar. I didn't think Jessica was a willing participant, so I reacted like any other man protecting his wife would. I grabbed the guy and nearly beat him to death, thinking he was forcing himself on her … only he wasn't. She had been seeing the guy behind my back for as long as we had been married." I take a breath. "I ended up going to jail for assault that night. They both pressed charges against me. She told the cops I hit her that night too, but I didn't. I have a fucked up criminal record now because of her."

Holly looks up at me. "Trip, that's … I don't know what I can say other than I'm sorry that you had to go through that."

I give her a sad smile. "It was a long time ago. I learned how to deal and move on from it."

"Is that why you're the way you are?" she questions softly.

"What do you mean?"

She sighs. "The first night I met you at the bar, you went from me straight into the arms of another woman. Then when you came here and kept coming onto me the way you did, and how you seemed like the type that never took anything seriously, I figured you only wanted to have sex with me. I labeled you as a player without ever knowing you because I never dreamed you had this other side to you."

"A non-player side, you mean?" I tease.

"That, and how smart you really are." She taps the binder lying on the counter top. "In the couple weeks you've been here, you've organized this place and helped point out all the spots where Dad was losing money. I can see you believe in this place, and want to help it succeed. That made me change my mind about you, and I even found myself thinking about you more and more often."

I smile. "Are you trying to say that you are falling for me, Holly?"

She laughs. "I don't know what I'm saying, but I do know that when you first came here I would've never pictured myself in this moment—wrapped in your arms after having the best sex of my life."

To hear her say some of the same things I'm thinking right now is crazy. "I know exactly what you mean. Ever since Jessica, I've kept my emotions on lock-down. I've never spent much time with a woman until you. Normally I just …" I freeze trying to refrain from sounding like a complete asshole.

"Normally you just have sex and then get rid of them?" She fills in the blanks.

"Yeah … that makes me sound like a shallow fuck," I admit.

She nods. "It does, but given what you've been through with your ex-wife, I understand why you're like that. I don't know what makes me so different, though."

"In the bar when I first kissed you, I'll admit I had every intention of sleeping with you and then walking away. I know that's harsh, but it's the truth. I saw you and I wanted you. I didn't even care if Max was with you or not. I planned on stealing you away from him, taking you to my hotel and having my way with you. But Max threw a wrench in that plan with he dragged you away. I stood there for a second, debating whether to chase you down …"

"But?" she prods.

"Another chick threw herself willingly into my arms and latched her lips on mine, so I took the easy way out. I figured Max was your jealous boyfriend and if I went after you there would be a fight. As much as you probably don't believe it, I try to avoid those at all costs. I, more than anyone, know how quickly a simple fight can escalate to the point where the law gets involved."

"Is that why you didn't hit Jackson back the other day?"

My nose tingles at the thought of Jackson sucker punching me. If things were different, I would've beat that little shit into the ground. "It is. When I was a kid, I fought all the time. I fought with my brother, other kids at school, whoever. All it took was someone to look at me wrong and I would go after them without a second thought. Spending time in jail, and then living on probation for a year, really opened my eyes and I realized that sometimes it's better to just walk away."

Holly shoves her hair back from her face. "She really screwed you up, didn't she?"

I sigh. "She did, but I try to focus on the positive side of things. If I hadn't gone through all the things I have in my life, I wouldn't be here, right now, with you. This" —I squeeze her in my arms— "is amazing. You're amazing. I can't explain why, but I'm happy being with you."

She snuggles into my chest. "Me too. All this time, I thought Jackson was who I wanted, but tonight, it's like I saw his true colors. He's not who I thought he was, but more importantly, lately he's not the man that's been on my mind all the time either."

I rest my chin on her head as I think about just how she's been on my mind too. "You've been thinking about me? Why didn't you say anything? Since that day on the couch, all I've done is dream about you. I didn't say anything to you, because you never mentioned it. You barely looked at me after that. I figured you regretted it and were doing your best to forget, which hurt."

She pulls away so she can face me. "I didn't mean to hurt you. I felt confused and I had to take a step back from you. I'm not the kind of girl that sleeps around and I wasn't sure I was ready for that with you yet. I felt a connection with you, and I'm pretty sure you felt it too, but part of me was still in love with Jackson. I had to sort out everything I was feeling for both of you."

I tuck a strand behind her ear. "I guess I can understand that. You were with Jackson a long time. Are you sure things are really over between the two of you? I need to know now because when I fall in love, I fall hard. I don't want you to give me yourself now, but then decide you still love him."

I swallow as I wait on her answer, knowing exactly how dangerous it is to open up my heart to someone again. Something I swore to myself I'd never do again.

Holly touches my face with her fingers. "It's hard to say this, but I'm over Jackson. I know now what we had wasn't love. I mean, real love wouldn't make you feel bad about yourself, or hurt you all the time, right? I guess what I'm trying to say is I'm still searching for the right guy."

I bite the corner of my lower lip. "And you think that's me?"

She shrugs. "I have no idea. I just want someone's unconditional love—something that's true."

I thread my fingers through hers. "Everyone wants that."

I don't believe I've ever said a more true statement in my life. I had always been a hopeless romantic until Jessica crushed the idea of love for me. Opening myself up to someone isn't something I believed would ever happen again—that is until Holly. There's something about her that feels like home and is safe, and she makes me want to love someone again. Being with her is changing me.

Chapter Eleven

"Radioactive"

Holly

Trip tugs his cell phone out of his pocket and glances down at it. "It's getting late. We should probably go in."

I swing my legs off his lap and place my feet on the floor while grabbing his hand. "Come on. We can go to my room."

A wicked grin spreads across his face. "Again? You're going to kill me on our first night together. You really *were* deprived."

I giggle and lead him towards the door, walking backwards in front of him. "I really was. Looks like we're just going to have to keep at it until this craving goes away."

He shakes his head and grabs me around the waist, pulling me against his body. "I don't think it's ever going to go away for me. I'm addicted. You're stuck with me."

I smile and grab a hold of his shirt. "I think I'm starting to like the sound of that."

"You do, huh?" He kisses my lips. "Me, too."

I nod and start to open my mouth to tell him exactly how much

I'm starting to like the idea of being with him when headlights shine through the windows. "Who is here this late?" I turn around and squint, trying to make out the make of the car that pulled up next to my house. When I recognize the car, my brow scrunches. "What in the world is Max doing here so late?"

"It's after one in the morning. Does he make a habit of showing up in the middle of the night?" Trip asks as I lead him through the door.

I shake my head. "No. Never. Something must be wrong."

My heart thuds in my chest as we get closer to the car and Max hasn't attempted to get out. The engine still runs as I approach the driver's side and peer into the window. Max is slumped over the steering wheel with his head resting on his arms.

I tap on the glass. "Max? Are you all right?" He doesn't respond immediately, so I knock on the glass. "Max? Answer me. You're starting to scare me."

This time Max slowly pulls his head up and turns in my direction. I gasp and clutch my throat as Trip yanks the door open. "Jesus!"

Max's face is swollen and covered in blood. There's not a single inch of his face untouched. "Max? Oh my God. What happened? Are you okay? We should take you to the hospital."

A million things rush through my mind while I wait on his answer. He obviously didn't wreck his car, so something else horrible has happened to him.

Trip reaches in the car and shuts off the engine. "Can you walk? I think we should take you to the hospital, Max. You look like hell."

"No," Max rasps. "If I go to the hospital, they'll want me to press charges."

Trip leans in and wraps Max's arm around his shoulders, helping him stand. "Who in the hell did this to you?"

Max's bloodshot eyes cut to me. "Jackson."

My mouth drops open and my hand rushes to cover it. "Jackson did this to you? Why?"

Max doesn't answer me as Trip helps him inside the house. Trip deposits Max gently on the couch while my head continues to spin. Why would Jackson do this to my best friend? I thought he liked Max. They always seemed to get along so well. Did he do this because he was angry at me?

Anger builds inside of me and I fight the urge to jump in my car and find Jackson myself. This isn't right. He needs to be punished for what he's done to Max. No one should be allowed to get away with something like this.

"Holly, can you get some towels and something to clean him up with? We need to know how bad this is. If he needs stitches, we have to take him to the hospital whether he likes it or not."

Max sighs through his fat lip. "No hospitals."

Trip shakes his head. "No promises, buddy."

I run upstairs and grab some towels and then head back to the kitchen. The first aid kit under the sink is dusty. The last time we had to use this was when Grace showed up here stoned out of her mind with cuts all over her body. Dad freaked out and went to work, cleansing and covering all her wounds, yelling at her for coming around here like that. It was one of the only times I can clearly remember him raising his voice to her. For some reason, her showing up here bleeding all over the place pissed him off far more than when she shows up in her regular state, begging for drug money.

I wipe the dust off and carry the box into the living room where Trip is sitting on the coffee table across from Max. "You should tell her."

I hand Trip the towels and the box. "Tell me what?"

Max shakes his head. "Nothing."

Trip narrows his eyes at Max. "Don't act like this isn't a big deal. Either you tell her, or I will."

Fear creeps down my spine as I sit down next to Max. The fact that Trip knows something about *my* best friend that I don't can't be good. I take Max's hand and cradle it in my lap. "What is it? I thought we told each other everything?"

Tears fill his eyes and when he blinks they stream down his face. "Not this. I never wanted you to know this."

My vision begins to blur with tears of my own and I take a ragged breath. "Please, Max. Tell me. I don't like seeing you hurt."

Max bursts into full-blown sobs and I instinctively wrap my arms around him and pull him into a hug. I glance over at Trip. His face is marred with concern. I stroke the back of Max's head and mouth to Trip, "Tell me."

Trip takes a deep breath and says, "This has been going on for a while. Jackson apparently saw fit to use Max here as a punching bag whenever he felt the need."

My eyes widen. "For how long? And why am I just now finding out about this?"

Max pulls back and wipes his tender face gently. "I didn't want to lose you, Holl. I knew you thought Jackson was some great guy and I couldn't risk telling you that he liked to beat me up on a regular basis. I didn't want to lose your friendship. You're my only friend. It would've killed me if you took his side over mine and never spoke to me again."

My heart cracks and I fight back my emotions to keep from bursting into a million tears. I'm such a terrible friend. If this is my chance to attempt to make this situation right, then I've got to take it.

"So you allowed him to continue to do this to you right under my nose and not say anything? Max, I would've dumped his ass and encouraged you to go to the police about all this," I tell him firmly. "Please don't ever be afraid to tell me the truth about something. I love you. You're my best friend."

"You say that now, but if I were to tell you about this a year ago when it started, would you have been so willing? He had you snowballed for so long. It was scary how much control he had over you."

I take one of the towels from off the table and open the first aid kit to pull out some peroxide. I soak the corner of the towel and go to work on cleaning Max's face. As much as I hate to admit it, Max is right. It's hard for me to believe this is real when I have the blatant proof right in front of my eyes. I can't imagine how difficult it would've been for me to fathom my sweet, loving boyfriend being such a monster. But there's no point in admitting that. It won't help anyone to worry about anything other than the here and now.

Max winces as I clean his split lip. "I'm sorry this happened to you. It wasn't because of me, was it?"

He frowns. "When you called and told Trip that Jackson just left you stranded, something snapped in me. I had to confront him, so I set out to find him and tell him what a piece of shit I think he is. He can treat me like shit all he wants, but not you, Holl. You don't deserve that."

A tear falls down my cheek and I shake my head. "Neither do you. We should go to the police. We can't let him get away with this."

"I don't want people to know. I'm ashamed I allowed him to bully me for such a long time. Plus, if I go, I'll have to give the details. Everyone—my parents—will know that I'm ..."

I pat Max's leg. "I'll be right by your side. You won't be alone. No one is going to love you any less when they find out you're gay."

"And I'll go with you," Trip adds beside me. "You shouldn't let this get swept under the rug, man. It's time to fight back and stop being that asshole's punching bag."

I finish wiping up Max's face and he leans his head back and closes his eyes. He's struggling. I know more than anyone how hard coming out to the world will be for him. Turning Jackson in for what he's done will get not only everyone in this town involved, but the press too. A star motocross rider assaulting a gay man will make headlines for sure. I can't imagine how hard this must be for him.

Max takes a deep breath and then opens his eyes. "I guess it's time I stop hiding who I really am."

I grab his hand and squeeze it. "You're making the right choice. Let's go."

Trip

Inside the police station, Officer Jones stares me down for a long moment before turning his attention back to Max. It's the tattoos that make them all nervous. The artwork on both my arms tends to have that effect on some people. I stand behind Max while he works on filing a police report and applies for a restraining order against Jackson. Holly is right by his side, just like she promised.

"So tell me, Mr. Moore, where did the assault take place?" the heavy-set officer asks Max.

Max runs his hand through his brown hair. "It occurred on the street outside of Jackson Cruze's house."

The cop twists his lip, making his mustache crooked. "You said you drove yourself away from the scene. What were your intentions when going to Mr. Cruze's residence?"

Max shuffles his feet. "They were to tell him off, I guess."

The office nods and writes a couple notes down. "So you went over there with a preconceived plan to start trouble with your assailant?"

Max shakes his head. "No, I didn't. He hurt my best friend and put her in danger. I had to confront him about that. He couldn't just keep getting away with hurting her."

"Is this young lady whom you're referring to?"

"Yes."

He eyes Holly and returns his gaze back to Max. "Was she involved with Mr. Cruze?"

"Yes, but I don't see what that has to do with this," Max replies.

The officer sighs and sets his paper down. "This appears to be a domestic dispute over this girl. My advice to you, son, is to not get involved in other people's business—even if you are interested in pursuing the lady yourself."

Holly shakes her head. "It isn't like that, officer. Max and I are best friends. There's nothing going on between us."

The cop chuckles to himself. "You might want to let Mr. Moore know that—looks like he took quite the beating defending your honor."

Holly folds her arms across her chest. "I'm glad you think that someone like Jackson beating up my gay best friend is amusing. I'm sure the media would love to know about the cop that didn't take the matter seriously, especially since Jackson is sort of a celebrity."

I grin as I listen to my girl give the cop what for. I love that she's feisty enough to stand up for herself. Of course I'll step in anytime she needs me, but she's doing a pretty damn good job of handling the situation herself.

The chunky cop clears his throat. "Just hold on, Miss. I never once implied this wasn't a serious matter."

"But you did when you were insinuating that we were just a bunch of young people caught up in a silly love triangle, which I promise you isn't the case. Jackson Cruze is an arrogant jackass who believes he can get away with anything. He's been picking on my friend for some time now, and it has to end. I had to practically drag Max down here. Look at his face. He got the crap kicked out of him and he was afraid to come to you people for help because he didn't want to be judged. We get him here, and not only do you judge who he is and what he stands for, but you don't take him seriously. You were about to blow him off, weren't you?"

Officer Jones holds up his hands, attempting to calm Holly down. "I'm sorry if I came across that way. Believe me, this is a serious matter and we'll get right on this. I promise you. We take hate crimes very seriously."

"Good," she replies. "Now let's get back to allowing my friend to press charges against Jackson. He needs to know he's not above the law."

I remain silent the entire time. It's good to know I have a woman who can defend herself. She'll need to be tough, especially when it comes to dealing with our crazy fans. Those women go a little batty sometimes. Both Lanie and Aubrey both have had their fair share of run-ins with them and it wasn't pretty, so I'm sure Holly will face that too.

Once everything is completed, we make our way out to the parking lot. Holly turns to Max and wraps her arms around him. "I'm so proud of you."

He squeezes her against him. "It felt good to do that, like a weight has been lifted off me. Thank you for encouraging me."

"You're welcome," she says as she pulls back. "Go home and get some rest. It's nearly dawn, so you'll have to explain everything to your parents soon."

Max nods. "It's time they knew the real me." His gaze cuts to me. "Thank you, Trip."

I raise my eyebrows. "Me? I didn't do anything."

"Yes, you did. You came into my best friend's life and changed us both." He smiles and then winces and touches his tongue to his split lip. "See you guys later."

I shove my hands in my pockets and grin as I watch Max walk to his car, get in and drive away. It's nice to hear that I've had just as much of an effect on them as they have on me. I like being here, and I love being with Holly. I can't even explain how she's doing it, but she's opening me up to a world of possibility again. Where it's okay to open my heart and feel something for people, without the fear that they'll betray and crush my trust.

Holly slips her arm around my waist and leans her head against my shoulder. "He's right, you know."

I throw my arm around her shoulder and stare down at her. "About what?"

She grins. "About you changing me, showing me how a really great guy is supposed to treat me."

I stare into her big blue eyes. "I'd never treat you wrong."

"I know you wouldn't," she whispers before kissing my lips. "I love how you're honest and straight forward with me. Apparently Jackson is a sneaky coward. I don't know how I never saw it before. I'm pretty disappointed in myself."

I tip her chin up so I can stare into her eyes more. "It's easy to allow love to cloud rational thought. I'm guilty of the same thing. If I would've allowed my brain to process what was actually going on in front of me, I would've known my ex-wife didn't really love me. So don't blame yourself. It's not your fault."

She sighs. "It doesn't make me feel any less guilty for what happened to Max."

"Max should've told you sooner and stood up for himself. You can't blame yourself for that. I'm just glad he *did* come forward and something is going to be done now."

"Me too." She grabs my hand and tugs me towards the Mustang. "Come on. Let's go home."

I grin, loving the sound of going home with her, and allow her to lead the way.

Holly doesn't let go of my hand. The entire ride home we shifted the gears together and then she pulls me behind her into the house and then up to her room. She opens her bedroom door and then bites her lip as she tugs my hand to come inside.

Her room is exactly what I expected. It's tidy and orderly, just like her. All of her clothes are put away and her bed is covered with a cream colored comforter. She sits on her bed and pulls me down with her. The look in her eyes tells me she didn't bring me in here to talk. It's the same naughty glint I saw back in the restaurant when I knew she wanted me.

I reach out and cup her face, kissing her sweet lips. If I had to imagine what heaven would be like, this would be it.

She shoves her hands in my hair, keeping my mouth on hers as we fall back onto the bed together. I snake my hand around her waist and roll, effectively placing her on top of me. Holly straddles my waist, and the erection in my pants stiffens even more. It's like it knows what's about to happen and it's just as anxious as I am to get inside her again.

This time, I'm going take my time with her and make sure she knows she's special to me.

I sit up so we're face to face, and dip two fingers inside of her dress and slide it off her shoulder, trailing kisses on her bare skin as I go. She sighs as my tongue darts out and I taste the flesh above her collar bone.

"Trip …"she says my name with a sigh as I mirror the moves on the other side.

The metal zipper on the side of her dress is warm between my fingers as I tug it open. Last time I was too impatient and didn't undress her completely, but I'm about to remove every scrap she has on this round. I shove the dress down around her hips before gliding my hand up the middle of her back and into her hair so I can pull her down into another kiss while my free hand unhooks her bra.

The silky-white material loosens around her as I remove those straps as well. Her full breasts fill the cups of her bra as I trace the outside edges, teasing her a bit before I finally pull it away. I dip my head and suck on one of her perfectly puckered pink nipples.

Holly bites her bottom lip as I stare up at her and lick a trail from one nipple to the other. Her breathing picks up as she brings her hand down to my cheek, to tip it up so she can kiss me. I turn my head into her hand and kiss her wrist. The delectable scent of her sweet perfume fills my nose. I close my eyes and relish in this moment with her. Before her, I thought I forgot how to love. I thought I was fucking broken, but she's showing me everyday that it's possible for me to love someone again. Every moment I spend with her, I grow a little more attached, and I feel compelled to do anything for her.

Now I remember what it was like when someone else was my entire world and can empathize with what Noel and Riff are going through.

"Is something wrong?" she whispers, staring into my eyes.

I shake my head and give her a reassuring smile. "No. Everything is absolutely perfect."

She grins. "I think so, too."

I pepper her face with kisses, elated to hear that she's feeling the same way I am. She begins to rock her weight against me, riding me through my jeans and her panties. Long strands of hair frame her face as she shoves my shirt up and then pulls it over my head. She tucks her hair behind her ear as she licks her way down my chest, stopping at my nipple to suck it in her mouth. The way she's looking up at me makes my mouth water. No one should be allowed to appear so angelic. It's not fucking fair to the rest of the world.

I cup her face and crush my lips to hers before plunging my tongue in her mouth. A sweet moan vibrates against my mouth as I feel how much I'm turning her on.

I tip her back, laying her on the bed, while I get on my knees in front of her. Both of my hands slide slowly up her creamy thighs before they find their way under her dress.

I give her my most wicked grin as I feel the bare skin beneath my finger tips. "I forgot I ripped your panties off before. Good thing I didn't remember that at the police station. I wouldn't have been able to keep my hands off you and concentrate."

She giggles. "Yeah. I stuffed them into my purse."

I eye the handbag sitting on the nightstand. "Maybe I need to keep that as a souvenir of the first orgasm I ever gave you."

She tilts her head. "Why do you need a memento? Are you planning on leaving me?"

I shake my head. "I'm not going anywhere, sweetness. Ever."

She grins and kisses me again. "Good."

My dick strains against my jeans, begging to be buried deep in her pussy.

When she tosses her head back, I drag my lips down her neck. "God, Trip. I don't think I'll ever get enough of you."

The sound of her needing me, asking me to take her is almost more than I can bear. I yank on her dress, tearing it a bit as I pull it over her head. I stare down at her completely bare and laid out before me. I've never seen a more beautiful creature in my entire life. A tug in my chest I haven't felt in my heart in a long time. I know it hasn't been that long, but there's just something about her that fits perfectly with me.

Holly sits up and unbuttons my jeans. I grab a condom from my back pocket and toss it onto the bed before I help her shove my jeans and boxers off my body. We both stare at each other, sitting there together completely naked. Her breathing is just as fast as mine as I reach for her.

I ease her back on the bed and then lay down beside her. I guide my hand down between her legs, before pressing a couple fingers against her swollen clit. "You're so fucking wet. I love how fucking excited you get when I touch you."

Holly's body writhes as I continue to circle her sweet spot.

"Oh, God," she pants. The sultry tone in her voice causes my cock to jerk.

"Are you going to come for me, baby?" I ask against her skin. "You're so fucking sexy when you come."

She whimpers and grabs my wrist as she comes hard against my hand. "Oh, ah … Trip."

"That's it, baby. Let go with me," I tell her.

I knead her tits as she returns from euphoria. I roll her taut nipple with my index finger and thumb. Watching her fall apart from the things I do to her body, causes an intense rush throughout my body, making it hard to hold back any longer from taking her very difficult. I love the fact that I'm the only man that's ever made her feel that good.

I grab her face and kiss her hungrily, eager to make her come again. An intense need flows through me to claim this girl. I always want this woman to be *mine*.

I suck a quick breath when Holly touches my face and says, "I want you inside me."

I shake my head. "There's one more thing I want to give you first."

Before she can say anything else, I begin kissing a trail down her stomach. I nudge her thighs open and then go straight to work on her still swollen clit. I flick my tongue against it and lapping up the sweet juices of her arousal. I penetrate her core with two fingers and I feel her greedy pussy clench around them.

Holly's body twists, and she shoves her pussy against my mouth and she pants my name while she comes for the second time.

I kiss the inside of her thigh. "I believe that's what? Number four for the night, and we're not done yet."

She giggles. "You're serious about that Orgasm King thing, aren't you?"

I grab the condom from the bed and open the package. "I take my duties as ruler very seriously."

She laughs for a second before she glances down to watch me roll on the rubber. The amused expression on her face turns serious as hunger builds up again in her eyes. This girl is insatiable—I fucking love it.

I grab her legs and yank her to me, so I can slide my cock between her wet folds. After it's coated in her juices, I guide my cock into her. The intense pleasure of it causes me to close my eyes. "Damn. This is fucking heaven."

I shove into her all the way to the base and then pull back out. She searches out my lips again as I begin pumping into her. "Trip ..."

She doesn't have to say another word for me to know exactly what she's feeling, because I feel it to—this crazy connection that we have.

My fingers dig into her hips as a warm tingle spreads over my entire body. I close my eyes, willing myself to make this last longer, but I can't, being inside her feels too fucking good.

"Fuck. Oh, God. I'm coming, baby." Edging into oblivion, my moves become ridged. The quickened pace causes Holly to dig her nails into my back as she falls with me over the edge. "So fucking sexy ... Shit."

I growl as I let go and release, swearing that God himself just showed me heaven.

A tremor shakes my entire body as I try to settle down. I prop myself up with my elbows and lean my forehead against hers as I try to catch my breath. "You're fucking amazing."

There's no way life gets any sweeter than this.

Chapter Twelve

"Kiss Quick"

Holly

We lie in my bed wrapped in each other's arms. The sun rising brightens up my room and I study the intricate tattoos on Trip's left shoulder and arm. I trace my finger over the patterns and read the words *Music is Life* on his forearm. I've seen it on his arms many times, but I guess I didn't understand how much he was into music until last night when he told me he used to be in a band.

I run my finger over the words. "I like this one."

Trip rotates his wrist to check which one I was referring to. "Me too. It's true. Music is in my blood. I love it. I don't think I could ever fully give it up."

I prop myself up on an elbow. "I love that you are so passionate. Why did you stop playing?"

He pauses for a long moment, like he's searching for an answer. "I still play actually."

"I'd love to hear you play sometime."

He grins. "I'd like that."

My eyes wander up his arm to the words *Black Falcon* written on his shoulder. I touch his skin where the inked words appear. "Isn't this a band's name?"

Trip's eyes widen and his body stiffens. "Yes."

I tilt my head. It seems kind of childish to get something like that permanently tattooed into his skin, but I've heard of people doing crazier things before. I guess if you love something enough to put on your body forever, it's a good way to always remember being passionate about something. I don't want him to think I'm judging him for that. I can see how nervous he is just by me bringing it up. "I didn't know you were such a huge fan."

He relaxes and smiles. "Yeah. I'm a big fan. Do you like them?"

I shrug. "I've only really heard that song you were signing in the office."

"*Ball Busting Bitch*?"

I laugh at how ridiculous the name of it is. "That's the one. The radio played that one out."

He laughs too. "Tell me something I don't know."

"Other than that, I've never really listened to any of their music," I admit.

"They're an okay band."

Talking about music and bands makes me wonder about his regular job. "I never did ask what band you worked for."

He bites his lip and tucks a lock of my hair behind my ear. "Believe it or not, I actually work for Black Falcon."

My mouth drops open and sit up quickly, pulling the sheet up to cover my bare chest. "Are you serious?"

He tucks his arm behind his head. "Yep. Why are you so excited all of the sudden? I thought you weren't a fan."

"I'm not." The possibilities of somehow using the bands fame to help promote the track rushes through my brain. "Are you good friends with the guys in the band?"

Trip smirks. "I guess you could say that."

"This is perfect! I know how we can save the track."

Trip raises an eyebrow. "How's that?"

I turn towards him. "Do you think they would come and play a couple songs if we set up a race here at the track? If we had a major band perform here, we'd draw all kinds of sponsors, press and riders from all over the world. It would be exactly what this place needs."

He bites his bottom lip, like he's considering what I've asked. "Is that what you want? You don't think the investor's money will be enough?"

I shake my head. "Not to put the business back on top. Besides, you said the drummer of the band you work for is the investor, right? He would probably love to see this place make money, so he'd convince the other guys to come here. What do you think?"

He sighs and touches my face. "If that's what you want, then I'll do my best to make it happen."

I squeal and hug him. "Thank you. This will mean so much to this place and to Dad."

He rubs my back as I pull back and kiss his lips. The simple peck between us turns passionate as he opens his mouth and slides his tongue against mine. My hands find their way into his hair and his hand slips down my back, shoving the sheet down until he reaches my ass. His strong hands grip my ass and he pulls me on top of him.

I'm afraid I'm becoming addicted to this sexy man.

The moment Holly leaves the room I throw my head back against the pillow.

Shit.

I've gotten myself into a huge fucking mess by lying to her all this time. I should've told her before who I was, but I was afraid she would never give me the time of day if she knew I was famous. She doesn't like people like me—words from her own mouth.

The moment the guys all come here, or the moment she Google's the band, it's all over. She'll either forgive me and we can move on, or she'll hate me forever.

I sit up and grab my pants from the floor. I dig my cell phone out of the pocket and dial Tyke's number. "What's up, baby brother. You ready to come back yet? It's boring as shit without you here."

I roll my eyes and fight back the urge to argue with him about the age thing, but don't because I know there's no time. "Hey, bro. I have a favor to ask."

Tyke sighs into the phone. "What kind of trouble have you gotten yourself into this time?"

"No trouble, but I do need something from you. Well, from all the guys."

"Oh? Should I be afraid to even ask what that is?"

I shake my head even though I know he can't see me. "I need you all to come here and play a couple songs. That's it."

"You know the other guys aren't going to want to leave their women right now. That's the reason we're on break in the first place."

"They can bring them, too. Holly and I want to set up a benefit, slash motocross competition here and we need something to draw people in."

"And let me guess, you want to use the band to promote your new little business?"

"Yes. What's wrong with that?"

"Nothing, I guess. Who is this Holly person you mentioned before?"

I bite my bottom lip and wish I could kick myself in the ass. I'm just beginning to figure out my relationship with Holly. I don't know if I'm ready to share what we are with my brother. "She's the owner's daughter."

"Don't forget to add the woman you're sleeping with," Tyke adds.

"It's not like that," I reply, my tone sharp. I hate the fact that my brother knows me almost as well as I know myself.

"Then how is it?"

I rub my face and allow my thoughts to travel to Holly. Her gorgeous smile comes to mind and denying what I feel for her to my own flesh and blood would make me a total tool, so I decide to give him the most honest answer I can. "I like her."

"Really? That's something I haven't heard you say in a long time. Matter of fact not since …"

"Let's not even bring her up," I beg. "Holly is nothing like Jessica. To compare the two wouldn't be fair."

Putting someone as straightforward and sweet as Holly up against my back stabbing, slutty ex isn't anywhere close to being even. Jessica isn't in Holly's league.

"That's good to know. The band can't handle you losing your shit right now. It's falling apart as it is, and it won't be able to withstand your ass getting carted off to jail over some girl you barely know."

I shake my head. "This is exactly why I don't tell you things. Every time I do, you always revert back to the past. I've grown up since then, Tyke. I'm not going to go around fighting every single asshole that looks at her three seconds too long. This track and Holly are both really important to me. I wouldn't do something stupid to screw up what I have going here."

"You're right. That was a long time ago, and maybe I don't give you enough credit for keeping your temper in check the last couple years." He pauses for a brief moment. "I've seen the way you tried to help Riff and Noel when they were going through their shit. It was very mature and insightful. I guess what I'm trying to say is, I'm sorry. If this girl makes you happy, then I'm all for you giving it a go with her."

I smile. "Thanks, man. So what do you say? You'll help me convince Riff and Noel to come out here for a weekend?"

"Of course I will. If this will help you make a new start in life, then I'll be there. You know you can always count on me, brother."

"Thanks. I'll owe you. I'll call you with the date as soon as I have one," I tell him before we say our goodbyes and end the call.

The bedroom door opens and Holly comes traipsing in wearing only a towel and a smile. My cock twitches at the sight of her, knowing how amazing it felt to be buried deep inside her last night. I can't help that my body craves that sweet, little pussy of hers now. It's going to be damn hard to get any real work done around here now with that distraction going on.

She smiles as she walks across the room to her closet. "See something you like?"

My eyes do a full sweep of her from head to toe. Her blonde hair still wet from her shower drips water beads down her bare back, while the towel opens on the side showing off her hip and thigh. Her beauty is unmatched by anything I've ever seen. "You're perfect and you know it."

Holly blushes and continues to sort through the rack of clothes. "Have you always been such a charmer?"

The urge to touch her skin overwhelms me. I push myself up off the bed, wearing nothing but a pair of boxer shorts and a smile. I stand behind her, pull her hair away from one shoulder and nuzzle my nose against her neck while grinding my erect cock against her ass. "It's you, sweetness, who has charmed this snake."

She tilts her head back and to the side, allowing me better access to her flesh. The scent of her floral shampoo and body wash fills my nose as I playfully nip at her neck.

She sighs as my tongue darts out to taste her. "You make me feel crazy, do you know that?"

"Is that a bad thing?" I mumble against her skin.

"It is when you're all that I can think about," she admits.

I spin her around in my arms and back her against the doorframe of the closet. "That makes us even then. I was just wondering how I was ever going to get any work done around here, knowing just how good you feel pressed up against me like this. All I'm going to be able to think about is being buried deep inside you again."

She swallows and then her mouth drifts open. I can tell she gets turned on when I talk dirty to her. It's impossible for her body to hide the way she feels. "I know exactly what you mean."

I press my lips against hers and tug on the towel until it opens up and falls from her body. Her puckered nipples rub against my solid chest as I deepen our kiss and thread my fingers into her wet hair. I'll never get tired of this with her. Every time I kiss her lips, all it does is drive me to possess more of this delicious taste.

My hand slides down her stomach and she whimpers as my finger finds her swollen clit. My finger glides around with ease and I suck in a quick breath. "I love how easily you get turned on for me. It makes me want to fuck you that much more."

She groans as I glide my finger inside her. "Trip. God. Ah."

Hearing her moan my name is enough to make me nearly come in my boxers. Sex with Holly is exciting. I love that she's not that experienced and isn't jaded by the experience like most of the groupies I've been fucking the past couple of years. Maybe that's why each time with her feels so fucking awesome.

I work my finger in and out of her until she's so frenzied she's clawing at my back. I love making her body feel good. It's almost better than when I get to come while deep inside her ... *almost*. The only thing better than that would be to fuck her raw and feel her wrapped around my dick like she is around my finger right now. "That greedy little pussy of yours keeps milking my finger." I kiss her lips. "Do you want me to fuck you?" My tongue darts out and I lick her top lip. "Huh?"

"Yes," she pants.

The way she's panting makes my cock rock-hard. I like that I'm the only man that's ever given her an orgasm and she knows I'm about to give her another one. Her body is begging for it. Anyone else causing her to react like this would drive me crazy. The need to claim her rages through my body. I want her to be mine. I want to be the only one who ever gets this part of her.

I trail my nose against her jaw and then whisper in her ear, "Ask me to fuck you. I want to hear you say it."

Her head falls back against the wood as I pull out and rub her clit a few times. "Oh, God."

I bite her earlobe hard enough for her to feel a little pain. "Say it."

"Please ..."

"Please, what? Say it," I command. "Say it and I'll give you exactly what you need."

"Fuck me," she says in a breathy voice. "I want you to fuck me, Trip."

I growl into her ear. "Good girl."

I slide my boxers down and kick them to the side, not wanting anything else between us. My cock springs free and rubs against her bare stomach as I pull her in for a kiss. Holly grabs the back of my neck and holds me against her as I deepen the kiss. She wants this just as much as I do.

I hoist her up against the wall and she wraps her legs around my waist. He wet pussy rubs against my bare shaft and I groan.

"Fuck. I want to feel you," I say against her mouth.

She bites her lower lip. "Have you ever …"

"Only a few times with my ex, but I've been tested since then and I swear I'm clean," I promise as I kiss her neck. "Have you?"

She nods. "Only once, before I left for school, but I've been checked too. It was a requirement to get birth control."

"So you're on the pill now?"

"Yes. I started taking them right before I came home from college."

I readjust my hips and she moans as the head of my cock slides against her clit. "I want you just like this."

She stares into my eyes. "Then take me."

With one swift move I push inside of her. The warmth of her surrounds me and I push in all the way to the base. I close my eyes and lean my forehead against hers. "Jesus. You feel so fucking good."

I pull back and fill her again. This time we both whimper with pure delight, which only propels me to move more. The best place on earth is right here. I'll never grow tired of this.

I work her pussy into a frenzy as I fuck her hard and fast against the wall. When my balls tighten, I know I won't be able to go on much longer. It feels too damn good.

Holly digs her nails into my back. She cries out my name against my lips as she comes undone in my arms while staring deep into my eyes. Witnessing her ecstasy and knowing that I made her come pushes me towards my own release.

"Fuck, Holly. I'm going to come." Before I have time to ask if I can come inside her or not, it's too late. I explode, filling her full. It was probably wrong of me to do that, but I couldn't help myself and my body wouldn't listen to my brain to hold off. In its own twisted way, I think my body took control and marked its territory. I kiss her face all over. "I'm sorry. I shouldn't have—"

"It's okay, Trip," she says, effectively cutting me off with a kiss. "I wanted you to."

I tilt my head and stare into her blue eyes. "You did?"

She nods and plays with the hair on the nape of my neck. "I didn't want you to stop. It felt so good."

I sigh. "I'm glad you're not mad at me. I promise to try and be more careful next time."

She grins while she's still tightly wrapped around me. "Who says there will be a next time?"

I bite her bottom lip. "Because I know how much you like it. I even got you to beg."

She smacks my shoulder, playfully. "Jerk."

I shrug. "You know you like me that way."

She giggles as pull out of her and set her on her feet. "Yeah … maybe I do."

She bends over to pick up her discarded towel and I smack her naked ass. "Hurry up and get dressed. We have lots of work to do if we're going to have a motocross competition with a special guest performance by Black Falcon here soon."

Holly rubs her ass and stands straight up. Her wide eyes show just how excited she is about my band playing here. "Oh, my God! You got them to say yes?"

My mouth pulls into a lopsided grin. "Of course I did."

She squeals and throws her arms around my neck. "This is fantastic. Thank you."

I stare down at her face and seeing her so happy makes my chest feel warm. I never thought doing something for someone else would make me so happy. It's here in this moment that I know Holly appreciates me as a person. Unlike most of the women I sleep with, she doesn't know me as the famous rock star that has lots of money and could be her meal ticket. This girl seems to like me for me, not what I can give to her. What is a simple gesture to me—asking my friends for a favor—seems to mean the world to her. It's then I decide once I make her see I'm a good man, despite my crazy past and celebrity status, I'm going to spoil her with a whole lot more. "You're most welcome."

Chapter Thirteen
"Same Old Trip"

Trip

Holly and I sit at the countertop in the front office, cuddling next to each other as she jots down a list of things we'll need for the event. We already have the basics down, like contacting sponsors and riders, but there is so much more to this business than I even knew. It's going to take me a while to learn everything. Thank God I have Holly here to help me with everything.

She pulls a Rolodex from under the counter and begins flipping through it. "Who are you calling?"

"We need riders for the event. The bigger the names in the sport we attract, the more money major sponsors will throw our way. We'll need prize money."

I scratch the back of my head. "How much do you think we'll actually need? Maybe I can get the band to donate."

She shakes her head. "We can't ask them to do that. They're giving enough already just by coming here and performing."

"I know they would contribute. It's not like they don't need the tax write-off, anyhow."

Holly bites her lower lip to try and contain her smile. "That would make things so much easier." The smile on her face turns into a frown as her line of sight trails off into the distance like she's lost in thought. "Trying to get money off larger companies is like pulling teeth. It's one of the main reasons Dad stopped holding events here. Once the attendance dwindled the sponsorships stopped too. There is no way the track can fund something like that on its own, and Dad doesn't have a penny saved up because Grace always figures out a way to take it."

It kills me to see her hurting like this. I wish there was a way to take the pain that she feels when she thinks about her mother away, but the past isn't something we can change. God knows how many times I wish I could go back and convince myself to not marry Jessica. She put me through pure hell, and I can tell Holly's mother has done the same to her.

What makes it worse is that I know Grace's fault Bill is ill. Eventually, Bill's secret will come out, and when it does Holly will hate her mother even more. Not saying that I blame her. From what I've gathered, Grace is a selfish woman. Holly is the complete opposite. Instead of always taking from people for her own personal gain, she gives. She quit school to help her father, and stopped riding dirt bikes because that fucker Jackson told her he didn't like her doing it. Giving up those two things alone proves she isn't a selfish person.

I take the pen out of her hand and lay it on the counter before threading my fingers through hers. "I think things are going to start getting better for you and Bill now."

Her eyes search my face. "How can you be so sure?"

I open my mouth to tell her everything—to tell her I have enough money to take care of her and Bill and turn this place into a Mecca for motocross. But the fear of rejection won't allow me to. If I tell her, and she hates me, I'm not sure I can recover.

I tuck a lock of her blonde hair behind her ear. "I'm going to take care of you, Holly. Anything you want, it's now my job to make sure you have it."

She smiles and leans her cheek into my hand. "You shouldn't promise me the world because when you say stuff like that, I feel like you can actually make that happen."

"It is the truth. I'll always find a way."

The sound of the office door opening startles me and I pull away from Holly just as Bill shuffles in. His shoulders sag as he makes his way towards his office, before plopping down in the chair at the desk. I know he doesn't want Holly to know just how sick he actually is, but by the looks of him, I don't know how much longer he can keep up the pretense his fatal illness will go away.

Holly stands up and slides the stool back under the counter as she leans against the doorframe of Bill's office. "You don't look so good, Dad. I think it's time you let me to take you to the hospital."

Bill busies himself with stacking a few loose papers on his desk. "I'm fine, honey. This will pass."

She folds her arms over her chest. "No, Dad. You've been saying that since I got home at the beginning of the summer. It's time to get checked out."

"No!" Bill yells and slams his fist onto the desk. "I'm not going anywhere."

Holly flinches and her face twists. Bill scrubs his hands down his face and then stares up at his daughter. Things would be so much easier if he would only tell her the truth. She'll understand—I know she will—then they can cherish the time they have left together. It's not fair that he's keeping something so huge from her.

"Bill …" I feel like outing him in front of her, but I quickly stop myself, knowing I'm keeping something from her too—something that her father has promised to keep secret as long as I keep his.

Bill's gray eyes shift in my direction and I know he knows exactly what's on my mind. "You got something to say, Trip?"

"I do, actually." Bill's eyes narrow at me, and I clear my throat. "Holly and I have come up with a plan to help get this place back on its feet."

He softens his gaze and tilts his head, clearly shocked that I didn't come out and tell Holly about his disease. "What's that?"

Holly's stance relaxes and she smiles and I can tell she's trying let go of the topic of forcing Bill to the doctor. "We're going to hold a motocross race here."

He leans back in the chair and smoothes his thinning hair back. "How do you propose we do that? We don't have the kind of clout needed to pull any big names here, not to mention the funding."

"We do now." Holly glances at me and smiles. "Trip works for a famous rock band called Black Falcon and he's got them to agree to come here and play a couple of songs. They will draw thousands of people, Dad. Trip thinks they might even be willing to donate money, too."

Bill chuckles and his eyes flit to me. "Is that so?"

Holly doesn't give me a chance to address her father's question. "Isn't that great?"

He nods. "Yes, and as long as Trip is helping you out, I have the feeling it's all going to turn out even better than you expect."

Holly runs into her father's office, no longer able to contain her excitement. She hugs him tight. "This is all going to work out, Dad. You'll see." She releases him and smiles. "I need to go out to the garage and see if I can dig up all the sound equipment. Do you think it's all still out there? We haven't used it in a while."

"It should be, but I think it's a good idea to get it all out and make sure it all still works since we haven't used it in a couple years."

"Oh. I hadn't thought about that." She frowns. "If it doesn't work that's just more money that we don't have that we'll have to spend."

Bill pats her hand. "I'm sure it'll be fine, honey."

"Okay. I'm going. Cross your fingers," she tells us as she turns and heads for the door.

The moment she's gone, Bill sets his sights on me. "You know this is going to blow your cover. It will be impossible for you to play in your own band and Holly not notice."

"She's going to find out sooner than that." I pick at my thumbnail. "The moment she gets on the computer to look up the band for promotional pictures it'll be over."

"Ah, yes—the internet. One of the beauties of modern day technology is you can find out information about anyone from the safety of your own home. Are you worried that she will no longer be interested in you once she discovers who you are?"

I sigh. "Yes. She told me herself that she would never date anyone famous."

"But that's before the two of you slept together."

My eyes widen and my heart jumps into my throat. "I ... uh ... um ... what?"

Bill rolls his eyes. "I may be sick, but I'm not deaf. We were all staying under the same roof last night ... and this morning. I know what the two of you have been up to."

Fuck. Nothing like the father of the girl you're sleeping with calling you out, although I will say he's rather calm about the entire situation. If some punk like me was shagging my daughter under my nose, I would kick his fucking ass. I know his laid-back demeanor has to be a front for what he's really thinking about me.

The best thing in this situation is to try and smooth things over. "Look, Bill, I apologize for that. I meant no disrespect towards you, or Holly for that matter. I guess I lost my head and didn't consider my surroundings. For that, I'm sorry."

He rests his elbows on his desk and folds his arms. "I can accept that. I remember what it was like to be young once. The thing I'm worried about is your intention."

"About what?" I question.

"I want to know what your intentions are with not only with this place, but with my daughter as well. Getting involved with her changes the dynamics of our deal a bit, don't you think?"

"It changes a lot," I agree. "But I still want to be in business with you, and I'm keeping my promise to pay for your medical expenses. Holly needs you in her life."

He frowns. "I know she does. That's my biggest fear—leaving her all alone. When I'm gone she won't have anyone except Max, and that scares me."

"You don't have to worry, Bill. I'll take care of her," I say.

"But you barely know her."

"I know enough to know she's a good person. She's loyal and selfless. If you ask me those are some damn good traits to have. To be honest with you, Bill, I've been looking for someone like her all my life." It's odd to hear my deepest, most private thoughts said out in the open.

Holly is exactly the kind of woman I've always wanted. I don't believe she'd ever betray me. It's just not her style.

Bill leans back in his chair. "I'm glad to hear you say that, because with this disease there's no promise of tomorrow. Knowing you and

Holly are together, and that you can take care of her even better than I can, takes a load off my shoulders. I have to know, do you love her?"

How can I answer that? Love? Is that even possible to know after only a few weeks' time?

When I don't answer right away, Bill says, "You don't have to answer that, Trip. Just do me a favor and think on it. All the best financial intentions in the world won't matter to Holly if you don't love her. She cares for you. I see the way she looks at you. You're the real reason she was able to finally tell Jackson goodbye and mean it. My daughter has been searching for real love ever since her mom ran out on us. She thought she'd found that in Jackson, but all that boy did was lie to her. I'm asking you to always be honest with her and don't lead her on if you don't see an actual future with her. There's something that happens to people who miss out on a mother's love. It triggers a never-ending search for unconditional love. So don't tell her you love her unless you really mean it. Lying to her will only hurt her more."

I swallow hard and nod. Toying with Holly's heart isn't something I ever want to do. It's the main reason I fought against my desire to sleep with her in the first place. She's the relationship kind of girl, and I knew that when I slept with her. Now I just have to figure out where she and I go from here. All I know right now is that I want to be with her. The rest I'll have to figure out. "I understand."

Bill smiles. "I know you do."

Holly

The next week flies by. Every moment of every day is spent working on organizing the race. Trip received confirmation back that the band will play at our race the very day he called them. Trip seems very excited that Black Falcon is coming here because he went to work getting graphics made for the signage for the event. Working alongside Trip has been great. Not once has he laughed at my ideas, or tried to take over like Jackson would've done if he'd been the one helping me.

We haven't slept apart since that first night we had sex. Sleeping with Trip has quickly become something I crave. Every little touch from him ignites a fire in my belly that only he can extinguish—something he is always eager to do.

I don't know what's come over me. I've been a complete horn-dog lately. Trip has a crazy effect on me. It's like I can't get enough of him. Even when he's with me, I'm constantly thinking of him, which is making my job confirming all the riders for this weekend difficult.

I press end on my cell phone and grin at Trip, who looks up me from his computer screen. "Charlie Chance just confirmed. That's one hundred and fifty riders in total for an open-class race. I think we've got enough bikes to have some great heats in the 125 and 250 classes."

Trip closes his laptop. "That's great news. One hundred and fifty is the goal, right?"

I nod. "Yes. It's the perfect number for our small race. The next one we do can go bigger. How's the budget looking?"

"It's completely under control. We've sold enough pre-order tickets to totally fund the event. This will give the track a great boost to get back on its feet."

"I'm excited to meet the band and thank them in person for all they've done," I say.

Trip sighs. "About that … there's something I need to tell you."

Pain appears in the expression on his face. I've never seen him like this. It's like he's being tortured with his own thoughts. I reach for his hand, willing away the hurt in his eyes. "Whatever it is, you can tell me. We'll work through it."

He sucks in his lower lip. "I'm actually—"

Before Trip has time to tell me whatever he was going to say, Dad bursts through the office door. "Trip come quick! Jackson is beating the hell out of Max. I'm not strong enough to break them up. I need your help!"

I suck in a quick breath as Trip flies off his stool and toward the door. I'm right on his heels as he comes to a skidding stop on the front porch. My eyes lock on the grotesque display of human behavior before me. Max lies on the ground in a curled up ball, while Jackson towers over him, shouting slurs.

My hand covers my mouth. I can't believe what I'm seeing. Jackson did an excellent job of hiding his true colors from me. I know Max told me how Jackson treated him, but never imagined I would witness this scene.

Jackson yanks his leg back and kicks Max square in the stomach before he bends down and says, "I'll give you something to really cry about to the cops, you fucking homo."

I gasp as Trip pushes forward and leaps over the banister, landing on Jackson's back. A cloud of dust engulfs them and they immediately begin tearing into each other. It's hard to tell where Trip ends and

Jackson begins. They roll around on the ground, both trying to gain the upper hand. Trip's size finally overpowers Jackson and he takes control.

Trip slams his fist into Jackson's face, and Jackson's head rocks back. "Why don't you pick on someone who isn't afraid to fight back?" Trip punches him again. "You fucking coward."

Trip's hands wrap around Jackson's throat as blind rage takes hold of him. I grab Dad's arm.

Oh God, please don't let Trip kill him. Jackson isn't worth Trip going back to jail for.

Jackson reaches up and shoves the heel of his hand into Trip's face. Jackson is having trouble getting air because of Trip's hold because his face turns beet red.

Max groans and rolls onto his back on the ground, just as sirens blare in the distance.

My gaze whips to Dad and panic sets in as I think about Trips past brushes with the law. I don't want him to get into any trouble over Jackson. "You called the cops?"

He nods. "I had to, honey. There's no way I can get involved physically. Besides, after what Jackson did to Max, the cops need to witness his handiwork. That boy needs to serve a little time."

The first thought that enters my mind is Trip's past. He's been in trouble for this sort of thing before. If the police show up and see this, his past may cause him major problems.

I rush off the porch and my dad yells for me to stop, but I don't listen. My own safety isn't important right now. I reach Trip just as I hear a car coming down the long gravel driveway. He's so focused on hurting Jackson that he's oblivious to everything else going on around him.

I grab his arm and pull. "Trip, let him go. The cops are coming.

They can't see you like this."

It takes a couple more hard tugs before he realizes I'm right there with him. "Holly, get back. I don't want you to get hurt."

I shake my head furiously. "No. Not until you back away from him. He's not worth it, Trip. Come on. Please," I beg.

Trip's gaze shoots from me to Jackson and then back to me before he releases his fingers. Jackson gasps for air and begins to cough, while Trip stares down at his hands. "What the hell am I doing?" It's almost as if he's whispering to himself more than me.

I help him up to his feet just as a police cruiser skids to a stop in the gravel in front of us. A young male officer jumps from the car and leaves his door wide open as he slaps his hat on his head and approaches Trip and I, his hand near the gun holstered on his side. The distinct sound of hard-rock music blasts from the car, like the guy was pumping himself up on the ride out here.

The stocky cop is about half a foot shorter than Trip's six-foot height, but appears to be about the same age. The officer's brown eyes roam around, accessing the situation before his sights turn back to Trip and I. I stand behind Trip, clinging to his arm, while the cop determines if the tattooed man standing before him is an immediate threat.

The cop clears his throat. "I'm Officer King. What's going on out here?"

I open my mouth to explain, but Trip beats me to the punch. "This guy" —he points down at Jackson— "came out here uninvited and started beating on our friend over there for no reason."

Officer King nods. "I see, and I suppose you stopped it?"

"Yes. I couldn't stand by and let him get away with hurting my friend. Max has a restraining order against him. It should be on file."

Jackson pushes himself up at the same time Max does. I race over to Max and help him to his feet. "Are you okay?"

Max nods. "I think so. It's not as bad as last time. Thank God for Trip, huh?"

I hug Max. "I'm so glad you're okay. Maybe now the law will actually do something about Jackson."

"On your feet," the officer commands while glaring down at Jackson. "I need to see some identification from all of you." The guys all fish their wallets from their back pockets and hands Officer King their drivers licenses. "You all stay put while I run these through."

Max and I walk over and stand next to Trip, while Jackson keeps a safe distance, leaning against his car.

Trips clamps Max's shoulder. "You all right, buddy?"

Max winces and Trip offers an apologetic frown. "I'm okay. Thank you for what you did. I owe you one."

"Any friend of Holly's, is a friend of mine." He slings his arm over my shoulders and pulls me into him.

Max grins at me. "Your girl, huh? I always knew you had a thing for him. I should start a dating service with my mad relationship-predicting skills."

I roll my eyes. "You're lucky you're wounded, because that would've earned you a smack."

Max laughs and then winces as he grabs his ribs. "You know you love me."

Trip and I both chuckle. It's good to see Max hasn't lost his playful spirit, and my heart aches knowing he's been going through hell for so long and I didn't stop it.

A moment later, the officer returns from his vehicle with a mean scowl on his face. He hands Max back his license first and then turns to Jackson, "I'm going to need you to turn around and place your hands behind your back."

My mouth drops open at the same time Max says, "Holy shit."

"My thoughts exactly," I say as I watch the cop cuff Jackson's hands behind his back.

"You can't do this, you know," Jackson says over his shoulder to Office King, who is busy reading him the Miranda rights. "Do you know who I am? You won't be able to hold me long. I have money and lawyers."

Officer King tightens the cuffs and Jackson winces. "I know exactly who you are. Ask me if I give two shits that you're some dirt bike hot shot. We have pictures on file of what you did to Max over there. We've been looking for you. Seems you've been hiding from us over the last week. The guys down at the station will be happy to finally meet you, especially your new cellmates. They love meeting celebrities who hate homosexuals."

"No. You can't do this. Please," Jackson begs as the cop leads him to the back of the cruiser and shoves him inside. I chuckle when the door slams in his face.

The cop straightens his clothes and readjusts the hat on his head before heading in our direction. "We're going to take him in for violating the restraining order. Would either of you two gentlemen like to press charges against Mr. Cruze?" Both Max and Trip both shake their heads at the same time and Officer King sighs. "I figured you'd say that. Let me give you a word of advice. Even though he probably came here to start trouble with the two of you, he's going to claim he didn't know the two of you would be here and that you attacked him."

"But officer that's not what happened," I chime in.

He looks at me. "I know that, but it'll basically be their word against his. There's nothing in the restraining order barring him from coming to Mountain Time specifically, and he is a well-known motocross figure, a judge is likely to side with him."

"That's ridiculous," I say.

"I agree, but Jackson may want to go after Trip as well for financial gain. He probably knows you're worth millions. You should really keep that in mind Mr. Douglas and press charges first." Office Kings hands Trip back his license.

Trip? Millions? What? I'm so confused. People who manage bands don't make that much, do they? And how would this cop know how much money he makes?

I stare up at Trip trying to figure out exactly what he's hiding from me. Is he not who he says he is? Do I really even know him at all? I know he feels me looking at him, be he refuses to make eye contact with me. He swallows hard and works the muscle under his jaw. He knows I just caught on that he's hiding something from me.

Trip stuffs his wallet in the back pocket of his jeans. "I'll keep that in mind."

"I think I will press charges," Max chimes in next to me, pulling me out of thought. "I don't want to get in trouble for something *he* started."

Trip rubs his forehead. "Maybe you're right, Max, we should go file."

Officer King nods. "I'll meet you down at the station."

Max steps away from me and towards his car. "You guys want to ride with me?"

"We'll follow you," Trip says, not giving me a chance to answer.

Max nods and heads for his car to follow the police cruiser into town. Trip shoves his hands into his pockets and heads off to his car without another word. It's not like him to ignore me. Even when we didn't exactly get along he never did that, and he's being awfully quiet too.

My stomach sinks. Am I just a fling to him? Is that why he's been keeping secrets from me? I wrap my arms around myself and follow Trip to the car. Finding out the truth about the man I've been slowly giving my heart to scares me. This could change everything.

Chapter Fourteen

"One More Lie"

Holly

The Mustang hums as Trip drives us down the road. He still hasn't said a word to me, and I'm not quite sure what I should say. I replay over and over in my mind the way the conversation will probably go the moment I confront him. He'll either say that the cop doesn't know what he's talking about, even though he seemed to have a lot of information about Trip. Trip didn't bother to correct him either, which makes me lean toward the cop telling the truth.

The other thing Trip might say is that it's the truth and that everything he's ever told me is a complete lie and he has no intention of ever getting really serious with me—that he wanted to keep me in the dark while he slept with me.

I sigh and run my hand through my hair. Either way I need to know. "Are you going to talk to me?"

Trip flexes his fingers around the steering wheel. "About what?"

"You know exactly what. Are you going to tell me what that cop meant and how he knows so much about you?"

He blows a rush of air through his nose. "Can we talk about this after we get the Jackson situation handled? Everyone is already on edge and I don't want to add to it. After that, I promise I'll explain everything to you."

I stare at him for a long moment, deciding if I can wait that long to know. Not knowing what his secret is makes my mind conjure up a million different things.

He glances over. "Please?"

I sigh. It's not ideal because I want to know now, but if I don't like what I hear, I don't see how I can make it through all the paperwork down at the police station. "Okay. Fine. But as soon as we're done, we're talking about this."

He reaches over and takes my hand, raising it to his lips and kissing my knuckles. "We will. It's something I've wanted to tell you for a while now. I'll be glad when everything is out in the open."

Trip pulls into the parking lot of the redbrick building and cuts the engine. The cop we followed pulls around the back, probably to unload his prisoner. I hop out of the car and glance around until I spot Max heading towards me. The remnants of the last attack from Jackson still cover his face. The bruises have turned from black to yellow, and have nearly disappeared, but he's got a newly busted lip thanks to Jackson. I'm ashamed all this happened to him, but one good thing came out of it. Max's parents finally found out that he's gay. His deepest secret that he never wanted them to know is finally out in the open and the reaction Max feared never came. Both of his parents fully accepted the fact that their son was gay, and said they had suspected so for a long time. Max has been the happiest I've ever seen him. That is, until just a little while ago when he was reminded that not all people are so open-minded.

Trip rushes over and wraps his arm around my shoulders and says to Max, "Let's go end this."

Fluorescent lights illuminate the light-green brick walls inside the building. The three of us make our way to the front desk—the same one we were at when Max last filed a report.

The same heavy-set cop with the mustache greets us at the front desk. "You three back again?"

"Yes, sir. We're here to press charges against the guy that we got the restraining order for last week," Trip informs him.

The officer types a few words into his computer. "Ah, yes. Mr. Cruze. I see they just brought him in. Go ahead and tell me what happened."

I listen as both Max and Trip recount what took place leading up to the fight. I'm so proud of Max as I listen to him bravely tell the officer everything Jackson said to him. I'm glad he's finally standing up for himself.

Trip on the other hand seems rather angry and annoyed talking about Jackson. I can tell pushing the issue of the fight isn't something he really wants, but feels obligated to do.

"Let me get all this filed. Go ahead and have a seat." He nods toward the row of plastic chairs against the wall.

"Wonder how long this is going to take," Max says with mild annoyance in his voice. "I want to get this over with."

Just as I attempt to comfort Max, I hear my name being called from across the room. "Holly. Hey, Holly!"

I whip my head towards the frantic voice and my eyes widen as I watch an officer walk Grace up to a desk parallel to the reception desk. Her dirty-blonde hair is matted into clumps and the dingy-white tank-top she's wearing falls off her left shoulder. She looks like hell, and God knows she probably hasn't eaten or showered in days. The urge to

181

not acknowledge my mother's existence washes through me. It hurts to see her. It's a reminder that she loves drugs more than me.

Whatever she did to land herself in here is deserved. Besides, she should be used to this by now. I can't even begin to count the number of collect phone calls Dad receives from this place.

I turn to walk away without saying a word, pulling Trip along with me, but what she says stops me in my tracks. "Holly, please! Don't let me die in here. They're going to lock me up for a while this time. I need bail money. Call Bill. He'll get me out."

I spin on my heel. "Detoxing won't kill you, Grace. It'll do you some good to be in here for a while and get clean. Don't call the house this time. Dad doesn't need to get involved in your crap."

Grace fidgets under my stare, and her cheeks sink in even more when she frowns while she rocks back and forth on her heels. "Please, Holly. I'm dying. I have HIV, and I don't have much time. Don't let me rot in this jail like an animal. I'm still your mother. Don't you care if I die?"

My heart leaps into my throat and Trip's arm tightens around my waist. Did I just hear her right?

"No." I shake my head. "You're lying. This is another trick to make me feel sorry for you. This is the same shit you pull on my dad, and I won't let you do this to me. You're already dead to me, Grace. Do you hear me? Dead."

She wipes her nose over and over while she stares dead into my eyes. "I deserve that. I'm a horrible person and a shitty mother, but you look like you turned out all right. Me staying away was the best thing. Bill knew that, which is why he still helps me. I swear to you that I'm telling you the truth. Bill knows all about it and refuses to let me die alone in a gutter some place like I deserve, but he won't let me come back home either." Grace sighs and wipes a couple tears out of her eyes. "He's forgiven me for making him sick. I hope one day you will too. I'm begging you to call him. He'll come get me."

My entire body tenses as her words sink in. This isn't real. Dad wouldn't do that to me. He wouldn't be this sick and not tell me about it. He has the flu or something—that's what he said. I'm not believing a word that comes out of her mouth unless I hear them straight from Dad.

Tears flow down my face and I drop my head, wishing they would just lock Grace up already. I don't want to stand here and listen to any more of her lies.

It's as if my prayers have been answered. I hear a male voice order, "Time to go, Pearson."

"Holly! Please let him know! I'm begging you!" Those are the last words I hear as my mother is carted off to a cell, somewhere in the building.

I don't know what's going to happen to her, and I'll probably go to hell for saying this, but I don't really care either. As long as she and her lies stay out of my life, things will be fine.

"You okay?" Trip whispers in my ear while he tugs me against his chest.

I sniff and attempt to wipe the moisture from my eyes. "Yeah. I hate her. I can't believe she would tell a lie like that. She's insane. I'm just ready to get out of here."

"Excuse me, officer? Can we go now or are we waiting on something?" Trip questions the cop.

The cop picks up the phone. "King? Yeah. The people involved with the Cruze case are set to go. Did you still want to talk with them? Okay." He turns his gaze to us. "Officer King will be right up."

Trip nods and he looks at me and shrugs. "Guess we can't leave yet."

My shoulders slump in disappointment. The longer I sit here, the longer all the unanswered questions I have from this evening are going to eat away at my brain. Trip and my father both have a lot of explaining to do. "I hope he hurries."

A few moments after Trip and I take a seat next to Max, Officer King comes through a door located in the back office. Next to the other officers in the room, I notice just how much younger he is.

King removes his hat and tucks it under his left arm while he holds some paper and a pen in the other. "I'm sorry to keep you. That Cruze guy is a piece of work. A demanding man, isn't he?"

Max chuckles next to me. "He's the biggest asshole I know."

"I won't say the biggest, but he's in the running." The cop sits down next to Trip and lays his hat on the empty chair beside him. "I know this is unprofessional, but I'm a huge fan and I wondered if I could get your autograph."

My brow furrows and I press my lips into a tight line as I wait for Trip's reaction. What in the hell is this guy talking about?

Trip pauses for a long moment, and then he removes his arms from my shoulders and reaches for the paper and pen. "Who do I make it out to?"

My mouth drops open and I stare at this complete stranger right next to me.

Trip

Fuck. This is not how I wanted Holly to find out about me.

"Make it out to Ben, please," Officer King says as I click the pen.

I scroll my autograph onto the blank piece of paper while I feel Holly's glare burning into me. She looks over my shoulder and reads the words I wrote:

Ben—

Thanks for rocking with Black Falcon!

Best,

Trip Douglas

I hand him back the paper and pen and rake my fingers through my hair. He smiles as he reads what I wrote. "Hell yeah. I'm framing this shit."

I throw up a metal horn and tell him, "Rock on, brother."

He quickly stands and slaps his hat back on his head. "I'll try to get them to hold Mr. Cruze as long as I can, but in all likelihood it won't be that long. If you can Mr. Douglas, I would keep your distance from him. Celebrity or not, your criminal record in this case isn't good. A judge will likely side with him since this would be your second offense in a domestic violence case."

Damn that Jessica. Will this shit continue to haunt my ass for the rest of my life? Cheating slut caused me to have a permanent blemish with the law.

I reach out and shake Officer King's hand. "Thanks, man. I appreciate the heads up."

"No worries. Call me up here at the station if you need anything else."

"Will do."

As the cop leaves us alone, I sigh, knowing it's time to face the firing squad. I turn towards Holly. Both she and Max stare at me like I grew a third eye. "I can explain."

"Work for Black Falcon, huh?" Holly asks with heavy sarcasm in her voice.

I swallow. "I know you're pissed. I should've told you before, but I had my reasons."

Max throws up his hands. "Wait. So you're in the band, Black Falcon?"

I nod. "Yeah. I'm the drummer."

"Fucking rad. Holly, didn't you know?" Max asks, surprised by my identity.

Holly's eyes widen. "You're Mr. Snare?"

I try to take her hand, but she pulls away from my touch. "I was going to tell you."

Her eyes search my face. "What else don't I know about you?"

"Nothing," I tell her firmly. "That's the only thing I've been keeping from you. I swear."

She drops her head and closes her eyes while Max and I sit quietly either side of her. "I need to get out of here."

"Come on. I'll take you home," I tell her.

"No," she snaps. "I'm not ready to talk to you right now. Max" — Holly turns towards him— "will you take me?"

"Of course," he answers automatically, before glancing over to me with an apologetic frown.

I open my mouth to protest, but quickly close it. I'm not ready for her to make the wrong assumptions about why I kept something so important about myself from her. I need her to know that I do care about her, despite my dumbass decision for not telling her sooner. Being rejected by her is something I don't think I can face.

Holly stands up next to me and I reach out and grab her hand and close my eyes. "I'm sorry."

"I can't do this right now, Trip." She pulls away from my grasp and my chest tightens as I open my eyes and watch her walk away.

The thought of never holding her in my arms again leaves me feeling cold and empty inside—a shell of the man without her. I'm tired of this empty feeling lingering inside me. The times I've spent with her the last few weeks have been some of the best I've had in a long time and that means something to me—*she* means something to me.

Right then, sitting in that sterile police station the realization hits me. I love her. It's not just the infatuation or great sex talking. I love her for her. I can't let this be the end. I know we're meant to be together. It's time I make her see that we're perfect for one another.

I jump up from the seat to chase after her, but I'm too late. All I see are Max's taillights driving away.

I need to bare my soul to this girl, and pray that she forgives me for lying to her and accepts me for what I am.

Chapter Fifteen

"It Is What It Is"

Holly

I prop my leg up on Max's seat and rest my elbow on my knee as he drives me home. What the hell is happening? Is nothing in my life the way I thought? Jackson is a fucking wacko, Trip isn't who I thought he was, and does my dad have an incurable disease he's been hiding from me?

Tears I can no longer fight back burn my eyes and my face crumples as a sob escapes me. This is all too much. I can't take it. There's nothing left to do but cry.

"Hey?" Max rubs my back. "You okay?"

I shake my head against my leg. "No."

The thought of losing everyone I've ever cared about in one day hits me hard. Dad is everything to me. The one person I can always count on to be there for me. What am I going to do if what Grace says is true and he's dying? I can't lose him. Suddenly there's no air and I find myself gasping.

"Hold on, Holl," he says as he pulls the car over. Once we've stopped, I hear the seatbelt come loose. Max wraps his arm around me and attempts to tug me into a hug, but I won't budge. "It's going to be all right."

"How do you know?" I cry. "Grace says my dad has HIV and Trip has just been using me. My life is fucked."

I give in and allow him to pull me against him. "You don't even know if what Grace said is true. Talk to your dad before you go into hysterics."

I nod. "You're right. I need to calm down."

We're silent for a moment, but then Max asks, "As far as Trip goes, I'm sure he has his reasons. Can you imagine what it must be like for him—everyone always wanting something from him because of who he is? He's probably tired of all that. You should be open to what he has to say before you pass judgment, Holl. He's been nothing but awesome to us … well, except for that first night in the bar. He was a little douchey to you then, but other than that … very cool."

I pull back and wipe my face with my hand. "You don't think he's just using me for sex?"

Max shakes his head. "Jackson was the one that was doing that, not Trip. If he were just using you he wouldn't have stuck around as long as he has, not to mention kicking Jackson's ass to help me out. Do you know how big of a risk that was for him to do that for me? He risked being exposed to save me from a beating, and he didn't even hesitate. If the press gets a hold of what happened it could trash his reputation and get him labeled as a loose cannon. That's a good man in my book."

This is true. Jackson would never have stuck his neck out for a friend of mine like Trip did, and we were together for two years. It still doesn't answer the lingering question in my gut. "But he's a fucking rock star. What in the hell is he doing wasting his time with me? He can have any woman he wants."

Max gives me a sad smile and touches the underside of my chin. "You don't give yourself enough credit, blondie. You're an incredible person. You're beautiful, smart, funny, and have one hell of a mouth on you. If I were straight, believe me, I'd be chasing you like crazy."

I laugh. "If you were straight, I doubt you'd be this sweet."

He chuckles. "You're right. I'd probably gross you out on a daily basis with my tactics to get into your pants."

"Eww," I say and shake my head. "Don't ever insinuate you want to get into my pants again. It's creepy."

"Deal." He pulls back and smiles. "You ready to go home now?"

I lean my back against the seat. "Yeah. I need to get to the bottom of everything."

"Things will work out, Holl. Have faith."

Max hugs me goodbye and wishes me luck as he pulls up next to my house.

I shut the car door behind me and stare up at the house I've lived in all my life. The light is on in the living room. Dad is no doubt waiting to hear about the details of what happened down at the police station. He has no idea that the scrap that took place here today won't be the main topic of our conversation when I come home.

If what Grace says is true, I'm not sure how I'm going to react. The thought of my father not being on this earth anymore is something I can fathom.

I glance around as Max pulls out of the driveway. The Mustang isn't here, which is a relief. I don't think I can deal with both issues at once.

I force myself up the steps and onto the porch. The doorknob is smooth in my grasp, but I can't bring myself to turn it. Fear engulfs every inch of me and I begin to tremble. Turning around and avoiding the entire situation crosses my mind, but I know I can't let this go forever. It's not in my nature to move on without resolving an issue.

Before I have the chance to open the door on my own, Dad opens it from the inside. "Holly?" His eyes search the gravel lot behind me. "Honey, why are you just standing out there all alone? Where are Trip and Max?"

"Max gave me a ride home and I'm not sure where Trip is." I stare over his shoulder into the house, and suddenly the thought of being cornered in there, hearing some possible life-shattering information, seems too much. I gesture to the bench seat on the porch. "Can we sit?"

"Sure." Dad steps outside, concern written all over his pale face. The shadows created from the porch light make his cheekbones seem even more sunken. My eyes study his unsteady gait as he walks over and takes a seat.

He's definitely weaker than I've ever seen him. I think deep down I stopped believing this was the flu a couple of months ago. No ordinary cold lasts this long. To be honest I was afraid he had cancer. Never in a million years did the idea that he might have a terminal illness that resulted from a sexually transmitted disease. But, I guess most people wouldn't consider that.

I walk over and take a seat next to him so I can position myself to look directly into his eyes. "I saw Mom down at the station."

He raises his eyebrows. "Oh? What was she doing down there?"

I take a deep breath. "She was getting booked again, but that's not what I—"

"Damn it," Dad mutters. "I told her I was out of money to bail her out. I'm going to have to figure out a way to get her out of there."

Just like Grace predicted. "Would you listen to yourself? Why can't you just leave her in there? She's exactly where she needs to be—

a place where she can't hurt herself or someone else. Grace needs to stay in there and get help."

Dad shakes his head. "We've been over this before, honey. I can't leave her in there."

"Why?" I challenge him, wanting him to admit what I already know is likely to be true. "Why is she your responsibility to take care of?"

"Holly ..." his voice trails off like he would like nothing better than for me to drop the topic.

"No, Dad. I'm tired of her using you and getting away with it. She's ruined this track with her constant need for money for her habit and when she gets locked up for them. I want you to stop saving her," I demand.

"I can't!" His eyes grow wide like he can't believe he just yelled at me. "Don't you see that I can't?"

Tears burn my eyes and I fear that Grace's lies maybe the truth. "No. Tell me it's not true."

Dad's blue eyes soften. "Did she tell you?"

My bottom lip trembles and my entire body begins to shakes. "So it's true. You really have."

"Yes. I'm HIV positive," he says and his face twists.

"No." I shake my head furiously as my body grows numb. "No! Why did you allow her to give this to you? How could she do this?"

I break out into a full sob as I clutch my throat. That selfish bitch. She can rot in that cell for all I care.

Dad grasps my hand in his. "We didn't know she had it until it was too late. She contracted it after she had an affair when you were just a toddler. We were still together at the time, and she wasn't aware that she had it. After the doctors told her she was HIV positive, she left us. Your mother has had to live with the fact that she's given us both a death sentence because of sleeping with someone outside our marriage. The day Grace left, she told me looking at you every day was more than she could take. She knew you'd lose both your parents because of her stupidity. That's why she got herself mixed up in drugs. Not that I condone her method of dealing with our reality, but I understand why she does it. The guilt takes a toll."

Tears stream down my face. This isn't happening to me. When am I going to wake up from this nightmare?

Dad squeezes my hand. "I know this is all hard for you to understand because you only know her as this low-life drug addict, but she loves you, Holly. She always has. She begged to come back home so many times, but I always refused because she couldn't give the drugs up."

"Did she even try," I whisper.

A solemn expression fills his face. "Many times. Grace was never one with strong enough willpower to resist something she really wants."

I search his face. "Why didn't you tell me once I was old enough to understand?"

"I didn't want you to know about our health condition. I didn't want you to live in constant fear that we were going to die. It's tough being a kid. You didn't need this burden on your shoulders too. I love you, Holly. I'll always want to protect you."

I throw my arms around his neck. The bones in his thin shoulder press against my hands. He's lived with this secret while it's slowly been killing him before my eyes. I wish he would've told me about this, but I'm not sure knowing earlier would've made this any easier. All I can do is cherish every single day I have left with him on this earth. "I love you too, Dad."

"I'm sorry you had to find out this way, but I'm glad you know. It takes a huge weight off my shoulders," he says as he pulls back and kisses my cheek. Dad's entire body shivers. "It's getting chilly. I have to head back inside. Do you want me to make you something to eat?"

I shake my head. "No, thanks. I think I want to sit out here for a while."

He pats my leg and shoves himself off the bench. "Take your time, honey. I know it's a lot to take in."

The moment Dad leaves my sight, and goes back into the house, I bolt from the house. Headlights shine on me as I fly across the parking lot. I run as fast and as hard as my legs will take me. My dad is my entire world right now, and everything about the house, the shop and the track remind me of him. I have to get away. I need to clear my head so I can process all this shit. My brain can't take much more.

The air whooshes from my lungs as I reach the field on the other side of the track and trip over a rock. The solid ground scrapes my arms and hands as I land hard, face first. That's when I can no longer hold back my tears. They flow like hot lava down my face and I roll onto my side and allow myself this time to grieve. And it's not just for my dad being sick, it's for the loss of my mother and how she's making me handle this all alone.

A hard sob escapes my lips just as strong hands wrap around my shoulders and lean me up. Trip is sitting on his knees in the dirt with his eyebrows pulled in and a slight frown in his face. The concern in his eyes chokes me up. He's the last person I expected to try and comfort me. After all, we aren't exactly on the best of terms right now.

I open my mouth to tell him to go away, but no words come out. Instead I wrap my arms around him and cry into his shoulder. The way he wraps his arms around me, like he's going to protect me forever makes me cry harder. Now that I know he's a mega-star, the reality hits me that he'll be leaving me soon too. I'll be left here completely alone.

"I've got you," he whispers and folds me in his arms even tighter. "I've got you."

"It's true. Grace was right." I cling to him like my life depends on it. "I can't lose him, Trip. He's all I've got."

"You've got me." He strokes the back of my head. "I'm not going anywhere."

"Don't make promises that you don't intend to keep," I say as I close my eyes and burrow myself into the crook of his neck.

Trip pulls back and cradles my face in his hands. "I'll always be here for you."

I try to pull away because the intensity in his stare is almost more than I can bear. "Trip … how can that be true? I'm a nobody and you're some famous rock star. You won't want to be with me forever."

"You're everything to me. Can't you see that you're *it* for me? You're perfect for me, Holly. I never understood love, not really, not until you. I like myself better when I'm with you. You and me—we're perfection," he whispers. "My feelings for you will never change."

My heart melts at the sound of his words, but the reality of how easily he could change his mind gnaws at the pit of my stomach. "What happens when someone better comes a long?"

His lips pull into a tight line. "There's no one on this earth that can compare to you. I *love* you, Holly."

I take a deep breath and close my eyes. The look in his green eyes tells me he means every word of what he's saying. I can't deny that I've had some pretty strong feelings for him too. How can I not tell him I feel the same way after he's laid out his feelings so clearly. He deserves my complete honesty after that.

I open my eyes to meet his gaze. "I think I love you too."

He grins. "Think, huh? That's a start, I guess. But just so we're clear, I *know* that I love you."

That causes me to smile and it feels good to hear that after so much crying and sadness. "I love you, too."

"That's much better," he murmurs against my lips before I fade into his kiss.

Chapter Sixteen
"Light Up the Sky"

Trip

Holly's dainty hand fits perfectly in mine as we walk around the track hand in hand. It'd taken an entire day of convincing, but she finally allowed me to dump some money into this place to get it ready for the race this weekend.

I throw my arm around her shoulders as we watch a crew repair parts of the track and build the stage for the band to perform. "This is going to be so awesome. I'm excited."

She smiles up at me. "Me too, but I still feel like it's wrong to allow you to spend so much of your own money on this place."

I kiss the tip of her nose. "I'm a partner, right? I look at spending my money here as investing in a business I co-own. You being my girl doesn't effect that."

She runs her hand down my back and raises an eyebrow when she grabs my butt. "Are you sure?"

I nip her bottom lip. "Afraid so, but you know that I would give you the world if you asked."

She grins. "Who knew the smart-assed player I met a month ago would be so sweet."

I chuckle. "Not me. I didn't know this part of me still existed until you brought it back out of me."

"I like knowing I'm the one who makes you so sweet." She rises up and presses her lips to mine.

"Okay, that's enough of that." Holly stiffens at the sound of my brother's voice and turns around. Tyke stands there in his dark jeans, and gray t-shirt, his blonde hair spiked in every direction. He shoves his hands deep in his pockets and smiles as he checks out my girl. "This must be Holly."

She tucks herself into my side and rests her hand on my stomach. "You must be Tyke."

Tyke's gaze cuts to me and he laughs before it returns to Holly. "How'd you know?"

She shrugs. "Lucky guess."

Holly's cell buzzes in her back pocket. After she checks the screen, she glances up at me. "Dad's calling. He's probably reminding me we have to get going to his appointment."

I nod and kiss her forehead. "Don't let us keep you. We'll be here when you get back."

"Okay," she tells me before turning in my brother's direction. "I guess I'll see you later?"

Tyke smiles. "You can count on it."

A light breeze blows Holly's blonde hair as she walks toward the house, swaying her hips. I can't take my eyes off her. She's like a magnet and the attraction between us is crazy. Man, I hate to be apart from that girl, but I love watching her walk away. Her ass has to be one of my most favorite body parts.

Tyke steps beside me and he turns to catch the same view I have. "Now I know why you haven't been returning my calls."

I laugh. "Sorry about that. I've been a little preoccupied."

"I can see that." He glances over at me. "It's good to see you happy again. It just sucks you had to find it on the other side of the country."

"Yeah." I sigh. "That's going to be rough. She'll never leave this place or her father. I wouldn't ask her to either. Leaving her here is going to be one of the hardest things I've ever done. I don't know how Noel and Riff do it."

"They'll be glad to hear that you're finally sympathetic to them needing so much time off," Tyke teases.

I rub my forehead. "I gave them a lot of shit for getting themselves tied down once it started affecting the band's schedule. It seemed insensitive to us because we still lived and breathed just the band."

"And now ..." he prods.

"Now I get it. I don't want to leave Holly here. Leaving her will kill me," I admit.

"You love her," his voice is as sure as the words he speaks. He's always known me better than anyone else.

"I do." I don't even hesitate when I answer because I know I've never said anything truer in my life.

Tyke nods. "It seems that we're all changing, going in different directions in life. I suspected this would happen one day. I just never imagined it would happen while we're still on top."

I furrow my brow. "What are you talking about? Short vacations don't mean the band is breaking up. You need to get that thought out of your head. We're all finding something else to love other than *just* the band and music. Don't you see that we're all finally starting to live our lives? No one is calling it quits."

I don't understand his line of thinking. My brother may be great at seeing the bigger picture in most things, but he's way off base on this one. No way will Black Falcon ever break up. That's just fucking insane.

Tyke gives me a sad smile. "I hope you're right, baby brother." He claps me on the back. "Come on. Give me the grand tour of your new business."

We spend the next couple of hours walking the dirt track, checking out all the rabbit hills, doubles and tabletop jumps. This place is really coming together. When you see it from this perspective, it really is amazing how much easier and quicker money makes things. Everything is newly painted and the porch on Holly and Bill's house is finally complete, along with the office being sandblasted. I even have a few computer nerds on the property hooking up new electronic equipment all over the place.

Shit is really coming together. Not only here at Mountain Time, but with Bill and Holly as well. The initial shock of Bill's diagnosis was hard for Holly, and I'm not sure she's quite over it yet, but I think once she gets involved in his medical care that will help. Holly is a fixer, so she'll want to know all the details about her father's condition and ways she can help ease his discomfort.

She's never once mentioned her mother to me again. I think there are some things a person just can't forgive. Maybe with time and a lot of soul-searching she'll figure out that situation on her own, but I'm not going to push her. It's her choice if she wants to reconcile with her mother. I don't know if I ever would if I were in her position.

I guess only time will tell.

As we're walking back toward the office, Tyke asks, "What's going on with the beats for the new tracks? Have you worked on them at all?"

I shove my hands into my pockets. "I've thought about a few of the songs, but I have to be honest, man, my mind has been on other things lately."

"Things as in Holly," he says filling in the blanks. "I suppose I should've accepted that. When we talked about her on the phone, I figured she was your main priority at the moment. Riff and Noel haven't worked on anything either."

The disgruntled tone in his voice doesn't go unnoticed. "Are you pissed? We still have loads of time. You know shit will come together and flow once we're in the studio. Don't sweat it."

"That's the problem, Trip. I'm the only one of us that does sweat it. I write the songs and ninety percent of the time, I'm the one who develops the melody too. It wasn't always like that. I remember a time when all of you wanted to chip in and put in the work to make the album kick ass." He scrubs his hand down his face.

I stop dead in my tracks and turn towards him. "Is that why you're really here so early—to lecture me about not working hard enough on the album?"

"That's part of the reason."

I flinch and let out an exasperated laugh. "You've got to be joking. Have you lectured the other two about this, or are you only going to single me out as usual."

"No, I plan on telling them too," Tyke answers.

"Good. If I'm going to get a talking to, then they should to. You should've been elected band leader. God knows Noel doesn't do much with his power except exploit it for his own personal gain."

He shakes his head. "No. I'm responsible for enough as it is and quite frankly, I'm tired of it."

Alarms go off in my brain. Fuck. I don't like where this conversation is leading. "What do you mean, Tyke? What are you not telling me?"

Tyke takes a deep breath and pinches the bridge of his nose. "I'm thinking of leaving the band."

"WHAT?!" My heart bangs against my ribs. I can't believe what I'm fucking hearing. "What the fuck do you mean? Wha—I don't … I mean … Damn it! Why?"

He frowns. "I'm ready to branch out and do my own thing for a while. I want to be able to perform the music that I write, the exact way I envision it in my mind."

I throw my hands up. "You can do that right now. Running off and starting over isn't the answer."

He tilts his head. "It is, Trip. This is something I've been thinking about for a while now, and this is the perfect time to branch out on my own. I'm not saying I'll leave the band forever. I just need a break, like the rest of you, only my break from Black Falcon won't be because of a woman."

Every fiber in my body buzzes with emotion, and for the first time in a long while, I feel like crying. "I'm begging you to not do this. It will ruin everything."

He places his hand on my shoulder. "It's all going to work out. You'll see. Thousands of bass players will line up to fill in for me. You guys won't even miss a beat."

I stare into my brother's eyes and see the conviction in them. He wants to do this. Who am I to deny him of his new dream? Nothing lasts forever, and I guess even identical twins need their own space.

I sigh. "When do you plan on telling the others?"

His lips pull into a tight frown. "I don't know. It's going to be soon, though. I think it may be after we record the new album. Don't say anything. I owe it to them to be the one to tell them."

I swallow down the lump building in my throat. "It seems like you've already made up your mind."

"I think I have. This is something I need to do."

"Then you should do it. It's not like we wouldn't take you back. You can try a solo gig and then come back after you've gotten it out of your system," I reason.

"Yeah ..." Tyke clears his throat. "We'll see."

Before we can delve any further into the topic, the Mustang pulls down the driveway. Holly liked that car so much I went ahead and bought it for her. You would've thought I'd given her the moon with how crazy she went when I'd handed her the title and the keys. It's an amazing feeling to have someone who appreciates me, so I don't mind spoiling her in return.

Holly helps Bill out of the car and waves to Tyke and I. I pull my hand from my pocket and wave at her in return as I think about how, in this moment, I finally feel complete. Too bad things can't stay like this. A shit storm is brewing, and it's all going to hit the fucking fan once Tyke breaks the news to our band brothers. Shit's about to get fucking real.

Chapter Seventeen

"Between the Raindrops"

Holly

I glance up from the registration table at the long line of riders here to sign up for the races this weekend. Every inch of the property at Mountain Time Speed Track seems like it has someone on it. Campers, sponsorship tents, scouts, riders, spectators, and our staff span out as far as the eye can see. Thanks to donations from Tyke and the rest of the Black Falcon guys we have been able to staff the two food pavilions, and hire a clean-up crew and experienced track hands. This place hasn't ever been this busy. If I weren't bombarded with getting everyone through this line as quick as I can so they can practice on the track, I would cry.

Screams erupt all around me as my boyfriend makes his way over. Trip shakes his head with a big grin on his face when he catches me staring at him. His black t-shirt clings to his chiseled chest and shows off the definition in his toned body. The tattoos covering his arms may give the impression of bad-boy, but I know now that there's nothing but a big softy hiding behind that filthy mouth.

Trip twists the baseball cap on his head backwards and bends down to kiss my cheek. "Hey, beautiful. How are you doing? Do you need me to help you?"

I shake my head. "The line will take three times as long if you sit here with me. People will line up to see you rather than register. So as much as I would like to take you up on that, I'm going to have to pass."

A random female fan yells, "WE LOVE YOU, TRIP!" from the back of the crowd somewhere.

I give him an I-told-you-so look and he laughs. "Good point. I'll send Max over to help you out."

I smile. "Good idea."

He kisses my lips. "I'll see you in a bit. I'm going to head over to the hotel and catch up with the guys. Tyke texted me a few minutes ago and told me Noel and Riff just made it in with their families."

"I'm nervous about meeting them," I admit.

He touches my cheek. "They're going to love you."

The crowd starts chanting, "Black Falcon. Black Falcon. Black Falcon." The noise is deafening.

"Is it like this for you all the time?" I ask as I shove a finger in my ear.

He nods. "Always. I've got to go, before they jump over this table."

"Go!" I shout to him over the crowd.

I can see he's reluctant to leave me, but we both know there's no way in hell he can stay out here and help. I push his arm and shoo him away until he finally turns and pushes his way back through the crowd.

I purse my lips and let out a long breath. This is some crazy life I've gotten myself mixed up in, but being with Trip is worth all the craziness.

The rest of the day goes on without a hitch. The riders made it through qualifying runs, and moved into the quarterfinals. This event is going better than expected. There are even a few scouts out there checking out the riders in this open class event.

After all the bikes clear out, and there's nothing but chatter from the campers, I breathe a sigh of relief.

We did it.

"Checking out your success?" Max asks next to me.

I cross my arms over my chest. "Yeah. It was pretty great."

"Agreed," he says while digging a small scrap of paper out of his pocket. He hands it to me. "Check it out."

I snatch the paper from his hand as he waves it in front of my face. "What is this?"

He chuckles. "Open it and see."

I unfold the paper, and a very male script is scrolled onto the paper asking Max to call him and then listing a phone number.

My eyes widen. "You met someone?"

Max grins. "I did. He's nice … and hot. I'm excited."

I laugh and hand the paper back to him while he practically glows. "I'm happy for you, Max. Everything is falling into place for you."

"And for you," he adds. "Trip and you are great together. I'm glad you ditched the asshole. Trip is so much better for you."

"He is. I love him so much." I give him a sad smile, not knowing if I can really ever forgive myself for not seeing the signs for how Jackson treated him for so long, but Max finally being in a good place is a start.

"I checked the county jail's website. Jackson hasn't made bail yet, but I'm sure he will. One of these days he's going to land himself in prison. I can't wait until we have our day in court and tell the world what a rotten bastard he is," Max says.

I take his hand in mine. "And I'll be right by your side."

He smiles. "Thank you, Holl. I'm glad I have a best friend like you."

A text message chimes in on my phone.

Trip: I'm waiting at your house for you. I'm excited you're meeting my friends.

I glance down at my track outfit and sigh. Going out tonight is the last thing I want to do, but if it's that important to Trip, I'll go.

Holly: See you in a few.

"Is that Trip?" Max asks.

"Yeah. He wants me to meet the rest of the band tonight, but I don't know if I feel up to it," I admit.

"Trip will understand if you want to wait." Max hugs me into his side and then clears his throat. "Have you heard from Grace?"

I stiffen in his arms. "She's called the house a few times and talked with Dad, but I'm not ready for that yet. I'm glad to hear she's handling detox well, and she may only have to serve six months of her eighteen month sentence."

Max pats my shoulder. "Maybe in time you will."

I shrug. "Maybe. She'll have to prove that she's changed before I even consider having any kind of relationship with her."

He gives me one final squeeze. "Okay, Blondie. I'll see you tomorrow. Go inside and get some rest."

I hug him back. "Will do."

Exhausted, I trudge inside the house. Trip is sitting in the living room talking to my Dad, who looks a little better since he started treatment again. The doctors where pretty pissed that he stayed away because of his inability to pay. They lectured him a lot about financial assistance, even though he won't need it now that Trip is covering his medical bills. I learned a lot when I went to the clinic with him the other day. There are so many false ideas floating around out there about HIV. The main thing I learned is that with correct medical care, Dad can live a long life, and that's exactly what I'm hoping for.

Trip glances up at me as I lean against the entryway into the living room. "You look beat."

I run my fingers through my hair. "I am."

Trip pushes himself up off the couch and comes to stand in front of me. He takes my hand in his. "We don't have to go to the hotel tonight. They'll all be here with their buses tomorrow. You can meet the other guys then."

Relieved, I smile. Meeting a bunch of rock stars and their beautiful wives isn't something I'm up for right now. "That sounds good. All I really want to do is take a hot shower and go to bed."

Trip wiggles his eyebrows. "Great idea."

I laugh as I push away from him, not wanting my dad to witness mine and Trip's public show of affection. "Good night, Dad."

"Night, honey. Great job today," he calls as I make my way upstairs with Trip in tow.

A few moments later, after Trip allows me to untangle myself from his arms, I step into a stream of hot water. I close my eyes and duck my head under the water, washing away the sweat and grime of the hectic day. My muscles ache from moving and carrying things all day long. It was constant today.

The shower curtain slides open and Trip stands there, wearing nothing but a wicked grin. "Mind if I join you?"

I laugh. "How can I turn down that proposal?"

He steps inside the shower with me and dips his head, allowing the water to flow through his hair. The water slides down his body and my first thought is *lucky water.*

I chuckle to myself for being jealous.

Trip cocks his head to the side. "What are you laughing about?"

I shake my head, still amused. "Nothing."

Trip leans in and presses my back against the tiled wall. "I think I'm just going to have to make you tell me."

I tilt my head up to stare into his hooded eyes. "How do you plan on doing that?"

He traces a finger down the center of my stomach all the way down to my pussy, where he slides it against the folds. I bite my lip as he toys with me, turning me on like only he can.

Trip presses his forehead to mine and licks his lips. "Like this," he whispers against my mouth.

The moment his finger rubs against my clit, I moan, "Trip."

"I fucking love the way you say my name." His tongue darts out and he traces my lower lip with it. "Say it again."

He rubs in a circular motion and my hands reach up, finding their way into his thick, black hair. I cling to him as I say his name again.

"Jesus," he murmurs before crushing his mouth against mine.

I'll never get tired of this, and I know it's crazy, but I can't imagine my world without him in it now. He's quickly becoming everything to me, and I can't wait to see where this relationship leads. Trip is right. We are perfection.

The Arizona heat beats down on us. It's ridiculously hot for an October day, but I'm not complaining. I would rather have the sunshine versus rain, which we get very little of. All of the riders that made it into the semi-finals are out on the track, preparing for their run, praying they'll make it to the finals where the bulk of the prize money lies in wait for the winners.

"Looks like it's going to be a kickass day for the heats," Trip says while surveying the tack beside me. "I don't think things could have gone better."

"I agree," I say, feeling completely accomplished, taking in the fact that Trip and I planned and pulled this huge event off together in less than two weeks. "We make an amazing team."

He reaches down and threads my fingers through his, before bringing my knuckles up to his lips. "That we do."

Black Falcon's tour buses pull into the gravel lot not far from my house and I let out a nervous sigh.

"Don't be nervous," Trip says.

I stare down at the simple t-shirt and jean shorts I'm wearing and envision the women on the bus looking much more glamorous than me. I'm not even in the same league. "Maybe I should change."

He furrows his brow. "Why? You look great."

Trip tugs on my hand and I freeze. "What if they hate me?"

He turns and wraps me in his arms. "Everyone on those buses will adore you, just like I do. You don't have anything to worry about. I promise."

I take a deep breath and stare at the buses. "Here goes nothing."

He laughs and leads me to the bus. Each step I take, my hands grow a little clammier. The fear of the unknown always gets to me. I've never have liked being in the spotlight or being judged and meeting a group of new people feels no different. All of them will be checking to see if I'm good enough for Trip, measuring me up against some standard I'm not likely to meet.

After a couple swift knocks on the door, Tyke opens with a grin. "Hey, lovebirds. Come on in. The others want to meet you."

"Great," I say and Trip gives my hand a little reassuring squeeze.

The second we're at the top of the steps, all eyes fall on me. I swallow hard, while Trip wears a smile so big it practically takes up his entire face. "Guys, this is Holly Pearson. Holly, this is everyone."

I stand there frozen for a moment, and then force myself to wave. "Hi."

A tall, slender brunette holding an infant in her arms is the first one to make a move. She places the baby's bottle on the counter and walks over to me. She smiles and extends her arm. "Hi, Holly. It's nice to meet you. I'm Lanie Falcon, Noel's wife." She motions to the very attractive man that was standing next to her. Like Trip, this guy is covered in tattoos and wears a beard.

I take her hand into mine and shake it, returning her smile with one of my own. I like her. She seems down to earth. The baby in her arms, wrapped in a soft blue blanket, squirms.

I smile down at the precious little thing. "He's beautiful."

Lanie's pretty face instantly brightens at the mention of the baby. "Thank you. He looks so much like his father." She laughs. "One of these days I have the feeling I'll be beating off the ladies with a big stick."

The beautiful redheaded woman sitting on the couch next to another hot guy with a crazy-looking Mohawk says, "More like a big club, Lanie."

The two men and women laugh along with Trip and Tyke. If the women are as crazy over the rest of these guys as they are over Trip, I would have to agree with the club theory.

Trip points to the second couple. "That's Aubrey and Riff. He's our lead guitarist."

Riff raises his hand and waves just as a second baby begins to cry from somewhere in the back. The tatted rocker grins and kisses Aubrey's cheek. "And that would be our daughter, Hailey. She gets cranky when the bus stops."

My eyes flit around the bus. Walking onto a bus with couples and babies isn't exactly the rock star image I had floating around in my mind.

There must be an odd expression on my face, because Trip asks, "Something wrong?"

"No," I answer, shaking myself out of the thought. "I guess this isn't exactly what I expected."

He chuckles and winks at me. "Yeah. We're a rowdy bunch of rockers on this bus."

Tyke opens the refrigerator door. "Do you want something to drink, Holly?"

"Sure. Do you have a bottle of water?" I ask.

Lanie and Aubrey look at each other knowingly and smile, before Lanie says, "I think Holly is going to fit in just fine around here. If she'd asked for a beer, she wouldn't have been the girl for you, Trip."

"Like I'd let the two of you decide that for me," Trip says with an amused tone.

"You're like a brother to us," Aubrey says. "We'll always watch out for you. We want to see you settle down with a nice girl—not one of those party-girls."

"Don't worry." Trip throws his arm around my shoulders. "My girl here isn't even a fan of our music."

I smack his stomach. "Shush, *Trip!*"

"What?" He laughs while his eyes twinkle. "That will earn you points with these two."

"That's true," Lanie confirms.

I shrug. "I've only ever heard one song."

"Which one?" Aubrey asks.

I grimace. "*Ball Busting Bitch.*"

Another round of laughter fills the bus as Noel begins shaking his head. "I'm never going to live that one down, am I?"

Lanie shakes her head and kisses his lips. "Afraid not."

"What's so funny about that song?" I whisper to Trip.

"It's actually funnier to hear Noel explain it," Trip replies.

"Yeah, Noel. Why don't you tell Holly about how you love to dedicate that song?" Riff says with a snicker as he returns, rocking a baby in a little pink blanket in his arms.

Noel launches into the story just as Tyke hands me a bottle and grins. "Welcome to the family, Holly."

And just like that, they accepted me into this down-to-earth group full fold. I might just fit in here after all.

Trip

I pound out the end beats to one of our hits on the foot pedal as I stare out into the sold out crowd. It's good to know this race has brought in enough money to put this place back in the black for a long time. Bill has thanked me about a million times this weekend while we watched the semi-finals and the final heats run through. He even allowed me and the rest of the Black Falcon members to award the prize money.

It's good to know everything is working out. I glance over and wink at Holly while she stands next to Lanie, watching the show from the side of the stage. Lanie and Aubrey plan on taking turns coming to the shows since they're moms now. They are built-in babysitters for each other since they are best friends. The arrangement works really well for them.

I wipe the sweat from my brow and take a quick chug of water while Noel talks to the crowd, amping them up for our most popular song.

Noel readjusts the guitar so it's resting on his back and pulls the microphone off the stand. He waves to his wife just before he says his trademark line. "This song goes out to the girl who shredded my heart back in high school. It's called *Ball Busting Bitch*, and Lanie, this one's for you."

I shake my head and laugh as I watch Holly's amused expression. We love to give him shit about the fact that he still has to say the line, even thought things have been great between him and Lanie for a long time now.

I kick up the base drum and hammer out the signature beats. Sitting behind all the guys is like watching their performance from the best fucking seat in the house. Noel's signature growl lights up the crowd, while Riff's saucy guitar licks, along with mine and Tyke's dirty beats, add sex appeal to the song.

It's funny how life works out sometimes. I've been through hell and back when it comes to love to finally find my own little heaven on earth. If things could always be like this, life would be fucking perfect.

I stare at the back of my brother's blond head, and sigh as I slam my drumstick into the high-hat, praying he wasn't serious about leaving the band. Somehow, some way, I'm going to have to convince him to stay—he's too fucking important. He's the fucking glue that holds us together.

I twirl one of my sticks in the air during the last few lines of the song to hype-up the show, before pounding the shit out of the bass drum and symbols as the last note is sung.

"You've all been a hell of a fucking crowd. On behalf of Mountain Time Speed Track and Black Falcon, we want to thank you all for coming out tonight. We love you all and we'll see you on the next trip!" Noel says, while pushing his sweat-drenched hair back from his face. "Good night, Tucson!"

I lay out five more timed beats and the lights cut off on the stage. The crowd of ten thousand people chants for the band to come back and play an encore, even after we finish throwing guitar picks and drumsticks out into the sea of people.

I step off stage and into Holly's waiting arms. "Wow. You were amazing!"

I grin down at her and pull her tighter into my sweaty body. "Thanks. So now you know what I do for a living, you think you'll be okay with it?"

She glances out into the crowd for a long moment before her gaze returns to me. "I'll admit that this is a little insane, but it doesn't change the fact that I love you. All these people just see you as a badass drummer. They don't know the real you, just the idea of you. But I know you. I know this." Holly places her hand over my heart. "I know it belongs to me, and I want you to know that this," she takes my hand and places it on her chest, "belongs to you."

"It's yours. All of it. Always," I tell her as I cradle her face in my hands.

"Then that's all I'll ever need," Holly says before I crush my lips against hers and we fade into our always.

Turn the page for a look at
Rock the Beginning
(Black Falcon, #0.5, Prequel to *Rock the Heart)*

Chapter One

Freshman year ...

Lane

So this is it. Freshman year.

I stand in the pristine hallway of Cedar Creek High School next to my best friend Cassandra Lutz as we survey the same faces we see year after year. Nothing in this town ever changes. I was hoping that I would be wowed in high school—dramatically swept off my feet on my first day by a dashing upper-classmen, living the dream of going to the prom as a freshman. Well, at least it's a big dream of mine.

But sadly, I'm disappointed yet again.

I sigh heavily and lean my back against the red locker and squeeze my books tighter against my chest. I can't wait to get out of here and run off to a big city where I can make something of myself. I've always thought a job in advertising sounded fun. Maybe I'll try that someday.

"Just once I'd love to have some fresh meat in this place," Cassandra says pulling her brown hair into a loose bun on the top of her head. "I hate knowing everything about these guys. There's no mystery. None of them do anything surprising."

I nod in total agreement. "Where are all the guys I read about in books—the ones that know exactly what to say? The first day of school is practically over and nothing remotely exciting has happened yet."

The moment the words leave my mouth, a crash against the lockers a few feet to my right draws my attention. I suddenly feel the urge to take back the last thing I said. This is not exactly the kind of excitement I was hoping for.

All the kids in the hallway stop dead in their tracks in unison and stare at the scene playing out before us like a bad teen sitcom. Roger Robertson, the guy we all know as the school bully, grips Wendell McFarland, a kid in my grade, by the collar of his shirt. Roger's large arms twist as he repositions his wrists in order to get a better grip, while he wears a sickening smile on his red, pimple-covered face. Roger isn't the kind of guy you want to mess with. His temper is about as red-hot as the flaming color of his hair and we all know he's been held back to the freshman level three times now. If Roger walks down the hallway, you get out of his way or duck for cover. His reputation of assholeism precedes him.

I instantly feel sorry for Wendell. His tiny, pencil-like frame is no match for the likes of Roger. "Give it up, you fucking pussy." I flinch as Roger yanks Wendell forward and slams him back even harder. "Don't make me tell you again. I know your parents are loaded. Cough up the dough."

Wendell gasps for air as Roger shoves his knuckles into his throat. "I don't have any money."

Another slam and Wendell's glasses slip down the bridge of his nose. "Cough it up you little shit stain."

My mouth gapes open and my eyes grow wide. It's painfully hard to watch. Someone has to stop this.

I glance around. Several of my classmates stand frozen. No one is making a move to stop this outright appalling display of human behavior. This makes me sick. What's wrong with these people? A desperate need to make this stop fills me.

Before I even realize what I'm doing I take a couple quick steps and open my mouth. "Stop it! Leave him alone!"

It's like a movie when a hush falls over the crowd. I know this isn't the smartest move, but I just can't stand by and do nothing. And, okay, I know the odds of me being able to stop Roger physically are about as good as a one-legged man in an ass-kicking contest, but I can't idly sit by. I wasn't raised that way.

Cassandra grabs my arm and whispers harshly, "Are you crazy, Lanie? What are you doing?"

I pull my arm from her grip and frown as I take in the fear in her brown eyes. I straighten my stance. I have to appear brave. "Someone has to stop this, Cass."

Roger's gaze darts from me to Wendell. His eyes are so brown they almost appear black and the pure venom in them causes my legs to shake. A deep laugh bursts out of his mouth and holds me in place. "What do we have here? Is this your little girlfriend, four-eyes? Is she here to save you?"

"N-n-no," Wendell stutters.

No one should be able to get away with treating people like this. "Stop it, Roger!"

Roger flings his gaze at me. "Or what, Shirley Temple? You going to make me?"

I stare down at the pink sundress I'm wearing. While very cute for my first day of school, it doesn't exactly scream badass. But this guy doesn't know what I'm capable of, so I can't let him rattle my nerves. "I might. Now, leave him alone."

Roger sneers while opening his large hands and makes a show of letting Wendell go. As soon as Wendell is free, he takes off running, without so much as looking back to make sure I'm not the one getting pounded now.

Thanks for the back-up, Wendell.

The bully turns to me and taps his lip. "Happy now, Shirley? I let him go, but it seems we have a small problem."

I lift my chin as Roger stalks towards me with slow steps, like a tiger stalking its prey. "What's that?"

"Someone is going to have to pay me. You see, I need money for a new tire and since you chased my little buddy off, I guess that leaves you to pay for it." He grins at me in a way a serial killer would … right before he murders his victim.

I grip my books tighter and my hands turn clammy. If he comes at me this Geometry book is going to make one hell of a weapon. "Fat chance. I'm not giving you any money."

He shakes his head as he steps in front of me. "That's where you're wrong. Guy, girl … doesn't matter to me. I'll still beat you into submission in order to get what I need, and what I need from you is money. You're going to get that for me. A nice girl like you seems good for it."

I narrow my eyes. "No, I'm not."

"Listen, bitch …" Roger slaps the books from my hands and leans in to me like he's about to attack, but a voice stops him.

"Pick those up." My neighbor and childhood friend, Noel Falcon pushes his way through the crowd. Once he's through, he narrows his eyes at Roger, daring him to cross him. "Pick those up, or I swear to God, you'll pay."

The guy in front of me takes a step back and smirks as Noel steps between us, using his body to shield me from Roger. At first I'm scared for Noel's safety, but I soon notice he's nearly an even match for the guy that's much older than him.

When did he get so tall and buff?

I guess I never noticed Noel's muscles before. The way they stretch his black t-shirt, and how broad his shoulders have actually gotten, has somehow slipped past me all summer long. Granted, I haven't seen him as much as I normally do over the summer. Noel was always busy every time I asked him to come over and go fishing off the dock behind my house like we always did, which was ... strange, considering we used to spend all of our time together.

His hair is longer too. The shaggy hair he sported last school year as he got into rock music would probably touch his shoulders now if he didn't have it pulled back into a low-set ponytail. I admit, he's looking pretty good.

Roger straightens his shoulders and rocks his neck like a trained fighter before he sets his eyes on Noel. "You'll walk away if you know what's good for you. This is between me and Shirley here."

Noels fingers fold into fists at his side. "I think you got that backwards, fucker. It's you that needs to beat it. No one messes with Lane. No one."

"Brave words. You're going to wish you'd walked away when I gave you the chance after I beat your face in," Roger sneers.

"I'll never walk away from Lane. You fuck with her, you fuck with me." There's a growl in Noel's voice I've never heard before. It's low and threatening. I never knew Noel could be so scary, or badass, or ... hot.

Oh my *God*. What am I thinking? Noel isn't hot. Noel is ... Noel, my friend—best friend since kindergarten.

I can't ponder on that last thought too long because Roger's laugh pulls me out of that bubble. Without warning Roger draws his arm back, launching it full force towards Noel's face. Two things happen so quickly that the scream building in my throat doesn't have time to come out. The first is Noel dodges the blow with ease and the second blasts Roger in the face first while simultaneously pushing me out of harms way.

I fall to the floor just as Roger tackles Noel and they crash to the ground. At first it appears that Roger has the upper hand until Noel uses some quick *UFC* style movements and turns the tables. Noel flips Roger onto his back and straddles him before gripping a handful of Roger's shirt in his hand and blasts a right hook into the monster redhead's face.

My mouth gapes open as the boy I've known most of my life defends me like no one else ever has.

A hand grips my shoulder and pulls me up off the floor. "Jesus, Lanie. Are you all right?" Cass asks. "Thank God Noel showed up when he did."

I'm about to agree with her just as the guys roll around in the hallway again and this time Roger's in control. Hell. No.

This weird urge to protect Noel comes over me. I fling myself on Roger's back without thinking about what I would do next. I wrap my arms around his neck and hold on tight. Not getting anywhere, I get desperate and grab a handful of red hair and yank as hard as I can. "Get off him!"

I ignore the distinct sound of tennis shoes scuffling on the tiled hallway as I tighten my grip on his hair. There's no way I'm letting anyone hurt Noel.

I'm pulled back but I refuse to release my hold on Roger. "Young lady, let him go!"

My head snaps in the direction of lanky man with thinning brown hair I recognize as being my English teacher, Mr. Jones. Then it dawns on me. Oh crap! I'm in deep shit. Dad isn't going to the let the fact that

I'm involved in a fight on the first day of school go without some sort of punishment. There's always the argument I was helping someone else that was getting bullied … even though that someone ran off and would probably be too scared to side with me against Roger. Surely one of these witnesses would attest to the fact this all began over Wendell, and that Roger isn't the innocent victim here.

I loosen my grip and Roger's hair falls free from my hands. "Crazy bitch," Roger mumbles under his breath. "Umph!"

I snicker as Noel brings his knee back down from Roger's groin, shutting him up completely. Roger falls over, cupping his crotch in the universally recognized, I've-just-been-nailed-in-the-balls style.

Noel stands and kicks Roger in the stomach one last time for good measure. "Don't *ever* talk to her that way again."

Mr. Jones sets me on my feet and turns to scolds the boys. "Knock it off and get to the principal's office." I turn to head in the opposite direction, thinking I'm in the clear because I'm a girl. "Not so fast. That means you too."

I stop dead in my tracks and turn slowly on my heel.

Damn. Can't blame me for trying.

Noel smoothes his hair back, tucking the loose strands behind his ear. He touches his tongue to the corner of his mouth and I notice a small cut on his bottom lip.

I tilt my head as I examine the rest of his face. "Are you okay?"

He shakes his fingers like he's trying to get rid of the pain from landing a couple punches to Roger's thick skull. "I'll be okay. What about you? I can't believe you had that in you to attack a guy like that. I haven't seen you go after someone since the third grade over a Barbie."

I shrug. "I couldn't let him hurt you."

Noel's eyes search my face and he swallows hard just as he takes a step toward me, nearly bumping his chest into mine. "I know exactly how you feel."

"Y-y-you do?" Where is all this nervous energy coming from? I've been in close proximity many times with Noel. Why does this time feel different—like all the air around us is charged?

"I said get to the office," Mr. Jones raises his voice causing me to jump and Noel wraps his arms around me. "You two need to get to the office while I finish helping Roger up. Don't make me tell you again."

Noel salutes the teacher and I giggle at his newfound anti-authority attitude. I pull away from Noel and turn towards the office. Our steps fall in line and he reaches down, threading his fingers through mine.

He's held my hand before, but never like this. This moment feels like the beginning of something beautiful.

Chapter Two
One week later...

Lane

The air is cool for a September night in Texas, but my entire body is warm and alive with excitement. I've snuck out of the house many nights before to meet Noel on this dock for a late night swim, but this is different. Things have certainly changed quite a bit over the last week.

Somehow over the summer we've gone from best friends to more. We've never really discussed this new territory of hand-holding and hugging that we've worked our way into, or what it means for us exactly. Maybe the subject will come up tonight.

People at school aren't surprised, I guess. Everyone knows Noel and I are close, so our new bouts of PDA don't raise too many eyebrows.

That doesn't mean we're ready to make our parents aware that our long-time friendship has blossomed into more though. They'd never let us be along together again.

I tiptoe down the hill to the dock behind my house and allow my eyes to adjust in the moonlight. At the end of the dock, Noel leans against the wood railing with his arms crossed against his chest, waiting for me. I'm not sure what tonight will hold for us, I just know I can't wait to see what unfolds.

A wide grin stretches across his face the moment our eyes meet. The features on his face are well defined like the new physique he acquired over the summer. His blue eyes shimmer with excitement the moment my feet hit the wood on the dock and my breath catches. Every time I see him now it's like my heart skips a beat.

I bite my lip and shove my hair behind my ear as Noel reaches his hand out to me. I slide mine into it without hesitation and my stomach flips.

He pulls me into his side. "I wasn't sure if you were coming."

I tilt my head. "Of course I was. Have I ever stood you up on this dock before?"

He swallows hard and pinches a lock of my long, brown hair before twirling it around his finger. "No, but things are a little different now, aren't they?"

I nod and my breathing picks up a notch. "About that … what are we doing?"

Noel's hand trembles a little as he releases my hair and touches my cheek with his fingertips. "I think it's pretty clear."

I know exactly what he's getting at, but I want to hear him say it. "You think so?"

He stands a little straighter and cups my face in his hands while staring into my eyes. "We're falling in love and finally giving into what fate has planned for us."

My heart thuds against my ribs. "Are you saying you love me?"

The grin on his face lights up my entire world. "You know I do. I think I've loved you since we were five. I'm just the idiot who didn't realize how much in love I was until this summer when I found myself getting jealous over any guy I caught looking at you. The feeling that you're meant to be mine won't leave me, and I don't know what to do about it, or if you even feel the same way."

"Is that why you stayed away all summer?" I ask.

"Yeah. I was hoping it would go away and we could stay friends, but all that went to hell that first day of school when I saw you and you needed help. I knew then I could never be just your friend. I'm always going to want more with you. I feel like you're my forever or something."

Emotions from within me take over and tears well in my eyes. "It might've taken me a little longer to come to the same conclusion, but I feel exactly the same way."

Noel's thumbs trace over my cheeks. "I love you, Lane."

I smile as a tear falls freely from my eye. "I love you too."

He leans in and presses his lips to mine. My eyes drift shut and I fall into his kiss—fall into him. This is everything I never knew I always wanted. His lips part and mine move in sync with his until he finally slips his tongue in my mouth. This isn't my first kiss, but it is the first time I've ever felt something kissing a boy. It's like tasting my future and I can picture my entire life in my mind—a life with Noel.

With more skill than I knew we both possessed, we slide down to the floor of the dock without breaking our kiss. I grip handfuls of his shirt and he teases the skin on my back just under the hem of my blouse. This is moving entirely too fast, but I can't find a logical reason in my brain to stop the madness. Being so close to Noel feels incredible and I don't want it to end.

Noel lies back, pulling me on top of him, allowing me to feel the bulge in his jeans against my thigh.

I'm scared as hell, but the way his lips move against the soft skin on my neck makes it a little less intimidating. "We don't have to go any further than you're ready for, Lane," he says, his breath hot and tempting on my flesh.

I press a feather-light kiss on his cheek. "I love you and I'm ready. We aren't strangers, and I can't think of one other person I would rather experience all my firsts with."

Noel tucks my hair behind my ear. "I want to be your only."

There's no fighting against that. That kind of magical romance is something all girls dream about. I'm just lucky I've found my prince so soon.

"I want you to be my forever," I tell him before he crushes his mouth to mine and we head into our forever.

Chapter Three
End of junior year ...

Noel

The drums pound out the last few beats of the song and I grin as I look at my band mates. "Yeah! I think we finally nailed it!"

Sam, the drummer taps the high-hat with his drumstick. "Finally! It only took us fifteen tries. You have to stop being such a fucking perfectionist, Noel, or we'll never have enough of our own songs to make a demo. We can't keep spending more than a month on one song."

"We need to have our shit together because after graduation next year we need to get on the road and find paying gigs like we talked about," I answer and then run my fingers down the thread of the guitar.

"We need to play more covers," Leon says, scratching the back of his shaggy head. "That's what people want to hear."

I stare at the two other guys in the band dumfounded. Sam pushes his glasses up the bridge of his nose and glances toward Leon as they wait on me to say something. Don't they see that originality is *everything* in the music business? Labels want bands that are different. We have to stand out and be the best.

I shake my head and smooth my dark hair back into my ponytail. "We're going to practice our own shit until our fingers bleed. We have to be on point if we want a record deal. Don't you guys want that?"

Leon shrugs and sets his bass in its case. "We do, but we aren't obsessed with it the way you are."

I open my mouth to protest, but Sam cuts me off. "Leon and I have been talking."

I narrow my eyes. "About what?"

Sam shoves his fingers through his bright-red hair. "We aren't going with you after graduation."

I shake my head. Unbelievable. These two jackasses are supposed to be my best friends—the guys who have the same goal as me. "We've talked about this!" I throw my head back and growl. "What the fuck, guys? I thought we were taking Thunder Dome on the road as soon as school's over?"

Leon sighs and his scrawny shoulders slump a bit. "I'm a senior, dude. My mom had me fill out some college applications, and I got into a few, some offered scholarships. I'm heading to Kentucky University next fall on nearly a full ride. I can't pass that up."

"Who gives a shit about college, man? We have a great thing going here with this band. We could really be something one day. Don't you want that?" I argue. Why would anyone pass on the opportunity to become a rock star? Choosing college over that is so fucking lame.

"I know you don't like it, Noel, but I'm applying to colleges as well. Music will always be there. You should think about going too, and maybe try once we get done with school." I study the freckles on Sam's face as he speaks and try not to completely lose my shit.

College will never be an option for me. Never. It takes me five times longer to read something than the rest of the kids in my L.D. class. Having Dyslexia hasn't been a fucking picnic in high school. Things get so jumbled in my brain and I know there's no way in hell I could make it through college courses.

I'm so glad Lane and I are on the same page about this.

"Whatever. You guys do whatever you have to do. I'm going on the road as planned as soon as we graduate next year. Lane will travel with me while I play solo shows until I find a band to hook up with." Both guys look at each other with an expression on their face that almost looks like pity and it makes my blood boil. "You know what, fuck you guys!"

"Noel …" Sam tries to stop me as I unplug my guitar and flip it around to rest against my back. "Don't be like that, man. We're just trying to be honest with you. Do you know what the odds are of us *actually* making it in the music industry? Slim to none. I'm just trying to be realistic. We need to go to college. It's the sensible thing to do."

I throw my hands on my hips. ""You know what's sensible? Following your dream when you have the talent and the drive. I know I'm going to make it. It's okay if you guys don't believe in me. Lane does, and she's the only person I need."

I turn to walk out of Sam's garage just as Leon says, "You don't know Lanie as well as you think. Seems to me like you two have different ideas about the future."

I whirl around. "What's that supposed to mean? I know my girlfriend—better than she knows herself."

Leon shrugs indifferently. "Maybe you do, but that doesn't explain why she was in the guidance counselor's office getting college applications today. Why do that if she isn't planning on going?"

I shake my head and storm out the door. "Whatever."

I rub the back of my neck as I walk towards my black Chevelle and pull the strap from around my neck and lay the guitar along the backseat. Surely Lane would tell me if she had doubts about the plan we've had in place since we became official our freshman year? She wouldn't just leave me hanging. We're forever, and there's no way I can spend years without her on the road.

I slam the door once I'm inside and fire up the engine. It roars to life and the only thing on my mind is finding out if Leon's claim has legs.

A few minutes later I park in Lane's driveway. This place has been like a second home to me since I was a little kid. I love her parents as if they are my own—another reason why we are perfect for each other.

The white Cape Cod with a red roof, shutters and door fits perfectly into the scenery next to Cedar Creek lake. It looks happy, like Lane. I love living on the water, and someday when I'm a famous rock star I'm going to buy a place on a lake for Lane and I to live in and start a family. She'll love that.

I knock on the door and step back as Lane's dad opens the door. He grins the moment he sees me. "Hi, Noel. How are you, son?"

I shove my hands in the pockets of my jeans. "I'm fine, Jim. Is Lane here?"

Jim scratches his dark bearded jaw-line and nods. "She's down at the dock, fishing, I think. You're welcome to grab a pole from the garage if you like."

"Thanks. I think I'll do that."

Jim steps out of the house, closing the door behind him, and pulls a set of keys from his pocket. "Let me unlock the man-door for you."

I follow Jim inside the garage. It's funny—as a kid I thought he was a huge man, but now at seventeen my height nearly matches his six-foot frame. Time really does change everything.

He hands me a black rod. "She should have bait down there."

After I thank Lane's dad, I make my way down the hill to the dock. There's always a certain level of comfort that falls over me when I come out here. Most of the major events in my life have taken place on this very dock—bonding with Lane, telling her I loved her, and even our first time together has all happened out here. This is most definitely our spot.

I lay my pole down and sneak down to where Lane sits on the edge, dangling her feet over the end. I place my hands over her eyes. "Guess who?"

She grins. "Um, Ryan Reynolds?"

I laugh and kiss her cheek. "Fuck Ryan Reynolds. You've got Noel Falcon, and I'm much better."

"I don't know ..." she trails off in a singsong voice.

"That's it," I growl and tackle her down to the dock and straddle her.

Lane squeals as I tickle her ribs and kiss her neck. "Stop! You're going to make me pee."

I laugh. "Never. Not until you tell me I'm the best."

She tries to catch her breath. "A little conceited, aren't we?"

"Only when it comes to you. I know I'm the best man for you."

She adjusts her back against the wood and I smooth her hair back from her face. "You'll get no argument from me."

I grin and lean in and kiss her lips. "That's good to know."

As much as I want to take this to the next level I know I can't. Her parents could be watching us out of their back window and that would be awkward for all of us. I pull back and push myself up so I can sit next to her.

After helping her back up to a sitting position, I grab my pole and begin to poke around in the tackle box for some plastic bait.

"How was band practice?" Lane asks.

I stiffen a bit, that this conversation will probably lead to an argument, and I hate when we fight. "Not good. The guys are both punking out on going on the road after graduation. Looks like it'll just be me and you." I cast my line into the water and I notice Lane fidget a bit. The best thing to do is get things out in the open. "Leon has this crazy idea that you don't want to go either. He's not right, is he?"

She doesn't look at me as she cranks her reel. "I want to go with you. You know that. But, I think maybe going to college first is a pretty good idea."

I roll my eyes. "Not you too. Come on, Lane. We've talked about this a million times. Don't you want freedom? The chance to go on the open road together before we have to face all that grown-up shit that people always bitch about."

Lane sighs. "It's not that easy, Noel."

"Yes it is, Lane. Do you want to be with me or not?"

Her head snaps in my direction. "Of course I do. Why would you even say something like that?"

"Because if you want to be with me, then we have to be together."

"Then why don't you enroll in a college with me."

I shake my head. "You of all people know I can't do that."

"I'll help you." She places her hand on my thigh. "We can get through school together just like we do everything else."

"Not college. I'm not cut out for it and I can't go. Not even for you." The words leave my mouth and I instantly regret them.

Lane's face twists. "You're an asshole."

She shoves herself up from the dock and takes off, sprinting towards her house.

"Fuck," I curse myself as I break into a full run to chase her down. She makes it halfway up the hill before I grab her from behind and spin her around in my arms. Her breath is ragged and her olive skin flushes.

"I'm an idiot. I'm sorry. You know I didn't mean it the way it sounded."

A tear streams down her cheek. "I don't get you, Noel. Is music so important to you that'd you'd throw everything we have a way to get it?"

I shake my head, but I know it would be a difficult choice. "No. You're all that matters to me."

"Then show me," she whispers.

I wipe away her tears with my thumbs before I press my lips to hers. "I will."

Chapter Four
One Year Later ...
Graduation Night

Noel

There are at least ten parties going on tonight and we're going to make our rounds, but first, Lane wants me to meet her on the dock for a private celebration. I grin to myself knowing this will be the last night we have to hide in order to have sex. This time tomorrow Lane and I will be out on the open road, making our way with no solid plan, going in whatever direction the music takes us.

I know she has her doubts. She expresses them nearly every day, but I know she doesn't really mean them. Once I get her out on the road everything will be fine. I just have to prove it to her that I can make it as a musician. I want her to be proud of me.

She's already waiting for me at the end of the dock. Her long brown hair falls in waves around her shoulders. The loose strands blow idly in the light breeze coming in off the lake. A tight jean skirt and cream colored shirt accentuates the deep tan she's already gotten even though it's only the beginning of summer. My girl is so damn beautiful. I'm a very lucky guy.

Excitement overtakes me and I rush down and scoop her up in my arms, lifting her off the ground. "We did it, babe. Can you believe it?"

She laughs in my arms. "I'm so proud of you, Noel."

I nuzzle my nose into her hair. "Not as proud as I am of you. You aced every single test they threw at you. You're a fucking genius. When I become a famous rock star, I'll pay for your tuition—anywhere you want to go."

"Noel—"

I cut her off, not allowing her a chance to argue with me. "Anywhere. I won't take no for an answer."

Lane frowns. "I can't let you do that."

I furrow my brow. "Of course you can. You'll deserve it. It'll make the little bit of struggle we have to go through at first totally worth it."

"Noel—" I cut her off again while I go on about the fancy house and cars I'm going to buy her, and she pushes on my chest.

I frown and set her on her feet. "What's wrong?"

Her delicate fingers rub her forehead before running through her hair. "I don't know how to tell you this."

I trail my hand up the bare skin on her arm and then stop when it reaches a strand of her hair. I wrap it around of my finger suddenly nervous about what she has to say. There's a slight quiver in her voice, and that's never a good sign. That only happens to her when she's nervous, and there's not one thing she should be nervous to tell me.

I lick my lips. "Whatever it is, just tell me. We'll get through it together."

Lane shakes her head. "This time we won't."

I take her face in my hands and force her to look into my eyes. "Lane, you're not making any sense."

237

She closes her eyes. "This is so hard."

I feel her tense under my touch as a tear falls down her face and my heart falls to the pit of my stomach. Lane never cries and it's something I can't stand to see. "Please don't cry. Baby, I'll fix it. Whatever it is, I'll fix it."

She opens her green eyes and stares at me, her eyes searching my face for answers. "Don't leave tomorrow."

I flinch. "The way you just said that makes it sound like I'll be leaving by myself."

"You will be if you go," she whispers.

I shake my head. "No. You promised you were going with me."

"I can't go with you, Noel."

I drop my hands from her face. "What do you mean, you can't? We talked about this since freshman year."

"Exactly," she cries. "We had no clue what we were talking about back then. Things change, Noel. I don't know why this is such a huge shock to you. I've been telling you for the last year that I want to go to college."

"I didn't think you were serious. Damn, Lane. Why are you waiting until just now to tell me this? We had a plan."

"*You* had a plan. Not me. Not one time have you asked me what I wanted!"

I close my eyes and pinch the bridge of my nose. "Yes I have."

"No. No you haven't. Have you heard anything I said about going to college and living in a dorm?"

"I heard you. I just didn't think you were serious." I sigh. "I can't believe you'd pick going to college over being with me."

"That's the same way I feel every time you pick music over me."

"I *never* pick music over you!"

"No? If I won't go with you, are you going to go anyway?" she challenges.

"Yes! Because that's been our plan." I raise my voice, completely frustrated by this blindside. "Music is my fucking life. You know that. It's all I have."

"You had me." Lane bites her plump, bottom lip as forces a cry back. "This is the end for us."

My heart squeezes so hard in my chest that panic starts setting in. "Please, Lane. Don't do this."

She kisses my cheek. "Goodbye, Noel."

My body turns completely numb as she turns and runs away from me. I should pull it together and go after her and force her to understand and try harder at convincing her to come with me, but I can't move. The idea that Lanie Vance is no longer mine hits me hard and I drop to my knees, shaking uncontrollably. I fist my hair in my hands and allow myself to cry for the loss of the only girl I'll ever really love.

Rock the Beat Playlist

It Will Rain—Bruno Mars

Closer—Nine Inch Nails

I Knew You Were Trouble—Taylor Swift

Rude Boy--Rihanna

Good Girls, Bad Guys—Falling In Reverse

I Wanna Be Bad—Willa Ford

Love Crime—My Darkest Days

I Said It—Nonpoint

Bringing Down the Giant—Saving Able

She Will Be Loved—Maroon 5

Gorilla—Bruno Mars

Radioactive—Imagine Dragons

Kiss Quick—Matt Nathanson

Same Old Trip—Chevelle

One More Lie—Aranda

It Is What It Is—Lifehouse

Light Up the Sky—Thousand Foot Krutch

Between the Raindrops—Lifehouse/Natasha Bedingfeild

Acknowledgments

First off, I want to thank you, my dear readers, for embracing this series and loving the men of Black Falcon as much as I do. Words cannot express how much you all mean to me. Love you all!

Emily Snow, Kelli Maine, and Kristen Proby (aka, The Naughty Mafia) this past year with you all has been amazing. Thank you for your love and support. Love you guys hard!

Holly Malgieri you freaking rock my world. Thank you for EVERYTHING you do for me. I couldn't make it on a daily basis without you. Your encouragement and undying support means so much to me. Thank you. Thank you. Thank you.

Jennifer Wolfel thank you for always being in my corner! You are the one person I depend on to give it to me straight. Thank you for your honesty and keeping me on task. Love ya!

Christine Estevez and Ellie (Ellie lovenbooks) thank you for standing by me and my books! It means the world to me. One word … VEGAS! Thanks for joining the Naughty Mafia team!

Aimee Pachoreck thank you for laying it out there for me and pushing me to be better!

Ryn Hughes you kick so much ass, woman! Thank you for

working with me through my crazy schedule. I always look forward to your red marks!

My beautiful ladies in Valentine's Vixen's Group, you all are the best. You guys always brighten my day and push me to be a better writer. Thank you!

To romance blogging community. Thank you for always supporting me and my books. I can't tell you how much every share, tweet, post and comment means to me. I read them all and every time I feel giddy. THANK YOU for everything you do. Blogging is not an easy job and I can't tell you how much I appreciate what you do for indie authors like me. You totally make our world go round.

Last, but never least the two men in my life, my husband and son. Thank you for putting up with me. I love you both more than words can express.

About the Author

New York Times and *USA Today* Best Selling author Michelle A. Valentine is a Central Ohio nurse turned author of erotic and New Adult romance of novels. Her love of hard-rock music, tattoos and sexy musicians inspires her sexy novels.

Find her:

Facebook:

http://www.facebook.com/pages/Michelle-A-Valentine/477823962249268?ref=hl

Twitter:

@M_A_Valentine

Blog:

http://michelleavalentine.blogspot.com/

Printed in Great Britain
by Amazon